MW01030068

Rusty NAIL

Book 6 in The Uncertain Saints MC Series

BY

LANI LYNN VALE

Copyright © 2016 Lani Lynn Vale

All rights reserved.

**ISBN-13:
978-1540395344**

**ISBN-10:
1540395340**

Dedication

As I was cleaning my daughter's throw up off the floor of her bedroom the other day, I realized a few things. Throw up, while disgusting, is still something that I wouldn't trade for the world. My kids are my life. My reason for writing. The inspiration behind every single child character in my novels. I love them, the good, the bad, and the gross.

This one is to you, babies.

Acknowledgements

Wander Aguiar- I love this photo. You took a perfect shot.

Jase Dean- I've wanted you on one of my covers for a long time. Thank you so much for posing for this photo. It's beautiful.

Danielle- one of my best friends in the entire world. Thank you for all that you do for me. I can never thank you enough.

Asli and Kelli- Y'all do so much and in such a short amount of time. Thank you so much for being there on a moment's notice.

Rusty Nail

CONTENTS

Lani Lynn Vale

Coup De Grace

The Uncertain Saints

Whiskey Neat

Jack & Coke

Vodka On The Rocks

Bad Apple

Dirty Mother

Rusty Nail (December 2016)

The Kilgore Fire Series

Shock Advised

Flash Point

Oxygen Deprived

Controlled Burn

Put Out (1-26-17)

I Like Big Dragons Series

I Like Big Dragons and I Cannot Lie

Dragons Need Love, Too

Oh, My Dragon (March 2017)

The Dixie Warden Rejects

Beard Mode (2-23-17)

PROLOGUE

Guess who got their life together! Not me. But someone,
somewhere, probably did.
-Coffee Cup

Raven

"Get your filthy fucking hands off her!" I screamed.

In fact, I screamed so loud and hard that I felt something give way in my throat, but that didn't stop me.

Especially not when I saw them tie July's hair to a hook about a foot above her head. The move pulled her head straight up, and forced her to keep it that way.

Even with a fucking sword right through her belly.

Her pregnant belly.

"Oh, God," I moaned. "Don't. Don't do it. She didn't mean to keep it from you. It was my fault. My idea."

My cries were ignored, and Jensen brought out a fucking knife the size of my forearm and walked up to July where she was being held up by nothing but her hair and the sword through her stomach.

The moment he was close enough, he stabbed July straight through her left wrist.

July screamed, and I screamed with her.

"Get it over with already. We don't need all this fanfare. We need her fucking dead. Do you really think this is necessary?" Barrett, my other captor, asked from his seat across the room.

We were in Jensen's brother's garage; his big rig truck, the one that'd transported me and July here, was just to the left of us.

The truck—void of its usual cargo trailer—smelled like cow shit.

Although, cow shit was a better smell than chickens; never again, in my life, would I ever complain about smells. Not after smelling what chickens smelled like up close and personal.

"This is necessary," Jensen said. "But, since we're in a hurry, I'll finish up here really quick."

He stabbed July three more times, once more in each limb, and then stepped back to admire his handiwork.

I must've made a sound, or made a move to draw their attention, because the next thing I knew I was standing up, my hair wrenched back so hard that I saw stars.

Nothing could compare to the pain that July was going through. The pain was evident in her posture, as well as her eyes when she managed to open them.

Oh, God. There's so much blood!

"I thought I told you to shut the fuck up."

With that he raised his fist, then slammed it down so hard against my face that my vision blurred.

Blackness started to dot the edges of my vision, and the next thing I knew I was dead to the world.

I woke up some time later, confused and disoriented.

And that was the first time I looked into those dark eyes belonging to a Wolf.

CHAPTER 1

A woman can only run as fast as her boobs will allow her.
-Fact of Life

Raven

"Oh, my God. What the fuck is it going to take to get that through your fat, thick head?" Jensen screamed on the tape that was playing in front of the courtroom.

I swallowed, looking over at my lawyer who was giving me a 'you're okay' nod.

I wasn't okay. In fact, I was so far from okay that I couldn't even factor this into a number, but I was going to make it.

There was a difference.

I had an end in sight.

I would testify to make sure that this man, this monster, never saw the light of day without having a razor-wire topped fence in his peripheral vision again.

This man would pay for what he did. To me. To the friend who'd been through hell with me, July. For the ladies before me that hadn't been saved.

Jensen would pay, and I was going to be the one to make sure he did.

I had the information that the court and jurors needed to make the correct decision. I had the strength to fight him.

I had rage fueling my determination, and I knew that if I could just get through this last day, then everything would be alright. I'd be able to leave this place and start anew.

"Alright," the judge said. "We've heard all this before. There's no reason to rehash things we've already gone over. If nobody has anything to add, we'll go ahead and dismiss the jurors to deliberate."

When nobody objected, the judge slapped his gavel on the wood circle on his desk, stood, and left before the bailiff could even tell anyone to rise.

The jurors were sent into the room behind them, and I took that moment to get the hell out of there.

There was no way I wanted to be anywhere close to the courthouse when the final verdict was read.

No sir-ree-Bob.

***

I knew he was there.

Before I even saw him, I felt his presence. It was like I had some sort of sixth sense when it came to this particular man.

"Leaving won't solve anything," Wolf, the brother of the woman who'd traveled through hell and came out on the other side with me, murmured.

I shrugged and loaded up yet another box into the back of my car.

It wouldn't fit. I knew it wouldn't. Yet, I had to try.

I was having to try quite a bit lately.

Try to get out of bed. Try to eat lunch. Try to leave my house.

I was afraid to do all those things.

A: I didn't want to get out of bed. When I got out of bed, reality pushed in. B: Eating lunch was what had gotten me there in the first place. I'd met Jensen while eating at my favorite restaurant. I'd thought we'd hit it off. I'd thought I finally found someone who I could be happy with. I was wrong. C: Leaving my house meant getting in the car. Getting in the car meant getting out of bed. Getting out of bed was hard on the best of days.

Therefore, I was tired of trying.

Tired of just about everything.

Except this man. This man standing in front of me wasn't a bad guy. He was a good guy.

He was a biker. A man who had principles. A man who was *taken*.

Taken by the beautiful blonde who was waving at me from the car.

I waved back, then turned to Wolf.

"Leaving is my only recourse at this juncture," I murmured. "If I don't leave, I just might get to a place that'll be a lot harder to get out of than this small town."

His eyes sharpened.

"What makes you think that leaving will fix that?" he asked. "It won't. I would know."

I laughed softly at him.

"I don't know if it'll solve anything but, at this point, it's not going to hurt to try," I replied. "It was very nice meeting you. I appreciate all the help you've given me over the last couple of months."

It wasn't just a couple of months. It was eleven months, three days and two hours since I'd been rescued.

My final good deed had been done. And, with only Jensen's sentencing remaining from this whole nightmare, I was free to leave.

Closing arguments had been given this morning, and I'd left before I could hear the verdict, because I couldn't handle knowing what he got. Nothing would ever be long enough as far as I was concerned.

"You know it wasn't a hardship," he murmured. "Nathan's going to miss you."

I smiled at the mention of Wolf's little boy.

He was a cutie, and someone from this small town who I'd definitely miss.

He's not mine.

That was another reason I was leaving.

These people who'd insinuated themselves into my life wouldn't be there forever. Eventually, they'd decide that what I had to offer wasn't worth the work it took to uphold a relationship with me.

I was beyond broken.

I was crushed.

There was nothing that could put me back together again.

"Hey!" Hannah, Wolf's pretty girlfriend, called from the cab of the SUV they were in. "Nathan has to pee! Let's go!"

Wolf lifted his hand up in acknowledgement that he'd heard, and then turned back to me.

"If you ever need anything, I'm here."

I smiled sadly at him.

My God, this man was beyond beautiful.

"I know, but I won't be calling. Thanks."

With that, I dropped down into the car I'd rented to get me to my new home.

New Orleans was my intended destination, but if somewhere else struck my fancy before I got there, I'd be stopping. Maybe to stay there for a few days. Maybe to make it my permanent home.

Who knew?

My eyes returned to the rearview mirror where I saw Wolf pull himself into the driver's side of Hannah's Jeep.

Hannah laughed at something he said as he got in, and my heart, what little of it there was left, broke.

***

Wolf

"What's with the long face?" Hannah asked.

I looked over at the woman I was seeing. The one who'd been able to pull me through some of the hardest and darkest days of my life.

I'd tell her today.

Today, I'd tell her that this wasn't going to work.

"She's leaving," I said as I drove Hannah's Jeep to her house, which was about thirty minutes from mine.

I'd thought that nothing could get better than the night I'd realized that Hannah had moved from Kilgore to Uncertain.

It hadn't been because of me. She hadn't even realized that I'd been living in the area at the time.

What had turned out to be a surprise on both of our parts had turned into instant awesome.

Except, over the last six months of us being together as a couple, things had just...fizzled out.

The spark that was once there was now just friendship on my part.

I wasn't sure what Hannah felt, but she deserved the truth, and now that I knew the fucker Jensen was going down for life with no option of parole, it was time to turn my attention to other matters.

Mainly to the fact that Hannah and I were together…but not really together.

In the six months that I'd been dating her, we'd yet to do much more than sleep in the same bed and spend time with each other.

We'd kissed just a handful of times and, truthfully, what we had resembled more of a friendship than a romantic relationship.

With my mind on other matters, I pulled into her driveway and immediately pulled Nathan out of the truck to set him free.

He walked to the closest tree and proceeded to pee on it.

"That's not fair," Hannah said with a laugh in her voice. "We can't do that."

I looked at Hannah and her daughter, and I smiled.

"No, you sure can't, can you?" I asked, tweaking Reggie's nose, causing her to giggle in the sweetest little voice I'd ever heard.

"Don't do that, Wolf!" Reggie growled. "Or I'll sic my Uncle Michael on you!"

I snorted and ruffled her hair. "We wouldn't want that, now would we?"

Reggie shook her head, face serious. "Of course you wouldn't."

Grinning at Hannah, I turned to survey Nathan's whereabouts before gesturing to Hannah to let them play.

Hannah placed Reggie on her feet, and she immediately ran to her swing set.

"Push!"

Nathan, of course, did all he could to push her, but all he did was manage to get her forward momentum going enough for her to come back and knock him off his feet.

Laughing my ass off, I walked to him and dusted him off, dropping down on my haunches to stare into his tear-filled blue eyes.

"You're okay," I told him.

He nodded. "I'm okay."

My heart clenched.

His father, my best friend since I was in grade school, was shining out of his eyes in that moment.

"I love you, boy," I told him.

He beamed at me.

At four years old, he was small for his age.

But his father had been small his entire life.

His kid was just like him.

"I love you too, Wolf," he told me somberly, tears still staining the tips of his lashes.

I grinned at him, my heart clutching slightly in my chest just like it always did when I saw him.

Nathan knew I wasn't his biological father.

I'd made it a point since he was small to tell him who his real father was. To tell him what a good man Garrett Cox had been, and what he'd done to change my life.

Nathan knew almost all there was to know about his father. The rest of the stuff, the good stuff, I'd wait to tell him until he was a lot older and could handle the stories—both good and bad.

"Go play, buddy. We're gonna leave soon, so you better get it all in now."

He nodded his head at me, then disappeared around the side of the play gym. A monster three story affair that Michael, Hannah's brother, and I had put up two months ago.

It was just about as good as it got for a kid, and I knew he wanted his own.

Something I planned on giving him soon—if I ever found the spare time.

"I need to tell you something," Hannah said softly from my side.

I gave Reggie a push and backed up until we were under the shade of a tree just to the right of the play gym.

"What?" I asked, keeping my eye on Nathan, who was now climbing arm over arm to the top of the rope that was dangling the length of the play house.

"I'm…we're…," she hesitated.

I looked over at her with a raised brow.

She blew out a breath.

"I'm not feeling you and me anymore," she blurted.

I grinned.

"You're not feeling us?" I knew where she was going.

Relief poured through me knowing I wasn't the only one who felt that way.

"Yes," she blew out a breath. "I…I've met someone…and I'd like to pursue something with, um, him."

"Oh, Jesus," I said, a smile on my face. "You're dropping me like a hot potato, aren't you?"

I'd stolen one of Reggie's lines, and Hannah's relieved smile let me know she understood me.

"I am," she confirmed. "This thing we have between us, it's good. But

Wolf, I think we both know it's just a friendship. I needed that friendship, and I still do, so I really hope that it will continue. It's just…I want to find someone who'll give me tingles."

My brows rose. "I don't give you tingles?"

Starting toward her, she held up her hand in worry. "You give me tingles. Just not the kind of tingles that lead to good things. Your tingles are more of an itch."

I snorted.

"Are we still going to go to the zoo next week?" I asked.

She nodded.

"Yes."

"Nobody's going to understand that we're just friends if we keep hanging out with each other," I noted.

She shrugged. "If they don't understand now, then they eventually will when we start seeing other people."

I sighed.

"So, who is this man that you have the hots for?" I questioned my friend.

She grinned. "You wouldn't know him."

"Try me."

"Okay." She backed up. "I don't know who he is. I've only seen him around town."

My brows rose.

"Now you really have me curious."

She blew out a breath.

"I know the feeling, I'm curious, too."

Lani Lynn Vale

CHAPTER 2

If it has tires or testicles, it's going to give you problems.
-Fact of Life

Raven

"Hey, Travis," I called to my boss. "Is there something I can get for you for lunch, or are you good?"

Travis looked over from his notebook where he was inputting numbers.

"I'm not sure," he said. "Where are you going?"

"We have a meeting today. Remember?" the other owner of Hail Auto Recovery, Dante Hail, called from somewhere behind us. Likely his office.

"Shit," Travis growled. "Is it with Peek?"

His question made him sound almost hopeful, and my curiosity was peaked.

Turning in my chair, a stack of prior repossessions in my lap, I studied Travis.

Travis was a big man. Tall with blonde hair, he reminded me of the quintessential high school quarterback. Travis, at first, was a lot to handle.

He said what he thought, and didn't try to hide what he thought about any given situation.

He was difficult to get to know, and if you didn't know him well, he came off as an asshole.

I would know.

He'd come off as an asshole to me five months ago when I'd shown up on Hail Auto Recovery's doorstep—out of gas and out of patience.

I'd run out of gas right outside of town and had started walking. A mile into my trip, I'd fallen and smacked my face against the asphalt, earning a bloody nose and a permanent scowl.

Then he'd taken one look at my bloodstained clothing, and he'd taken me under his wing.

He'd forced me to stay with him for the night, patched me up, filled up my car, and then offered me a job. An offer I'd taken him up on.

I hadn't gotten far from Karnack, Texas the day I'd said goodbye.

Just barely over the Texas/Louisiana state line, which happened to be where Hail's headquarters was located.

Lucky for me, I'd hit the asphalt with my face just a block away from the building that housed all of Hail's trucks.

Also lucky for me that Travis was there to catch me when I'd fallen out in a dead faint at seeing all the blood from my head wound on my clothes.

Dante, however, was nothing like his brother.

He was nice, yes, but he wasn't anywhere near as welcoming towards me.

He was much more suspicious by nature, and although I'd worn him down a bit over the last five months, he was still wary of me.

He'd looked into me, though, so he knew my past. Hell, I couldn't blame him for being wary.

I haven't lived an easy life.

I'd been in foster care since the age of four because my mother had died from a drug overdose.

By fourteen, I had run away from eight foster homes and had been sent to juvie four times.

By seventeen, I had gotten pregnant, lost my baby and dropped out of school.

By nineteen, though, I started turning it around. I'd gotten my GED, enrolled in college and had started working full-time.

By twenty-two, I'd graduated with my business degree and had started working when it all fell apart. I was arrested right along with my new bosses for supposedly helping them to launder money through their business.

By twenty-five, I'd given up on my business degree and had started picking up odd jobs here and there.

My luck, however, didn't hold.

Like some kind of magnet for them, I seemed to only meet bad guys. I had dated a total of four men, three of whom had gone to jail at some point during our relationship.

Jensen, however, gave me hope. He'd been the man who I'd thought was my turning point.

Then I'd overheard him and his friend, Barrett, speaking about kidnapping a woman and selling her to a man halfway across the country.

In my haste to get away from them, I'd inadvertently tripped some silent alarm they'd had installed in their yard, meaning they'd caught me before I could even make it all the way back to my shitty car.

Then, to put the icing on the cake, I'd been kidnapped right along with July, and we spent the next four months getting beaten and verbally abused. And raped, but I'm working through that.

That was where Wolf came in with July's now husband, Dean.

Wolf was my game changer. He was the man I would forever compare all future men to.

He'd literally changed my life, and although I wasn't going to see him ever again, he'd forever be in my heart.

He'd saved me from a life worse than death. He wasn't looking for me, but he found me. And I'd forever owe him.

"So, who are we meeting?" Travis asked. "I know it's not Wolf. He's not allowed here anymore."

The name 'Wolf' was pretty distinctive. I only knew one Wolf, and it was highly unlikely that this Wolf would be different from my Wolf.

Especially since I knew the Hails had problems with the Uncertain Saints MC.

Curiosity was always my downfall. This time, though, there would be no downfall.

Not for me.

I had too many strikes against me to add more to my list.

Wolf may be coming here, but I wouldn't be here when he did.

There had to be a reason Travis and Dante didn't like The Uncertain Saints, and I was going to make sure to keep my distance. I owed Wolf a great deal, but there was only so much shame that a woman could face, and I'd faced more than I wanted to.

"Alright," I said, standing and dropping the papers to the desktop. "I'm going to go have lunch and catch up on my reading since y'all are having meetings. If y'all need anything let me know."

With my back to the door and my eyes to Travis, whom I could see in his office, I knew Dante, who I couldn't see but I'd bet was watching me on the monitor like he always did. I backed away.

I'd nearly made it all the way to the door, too, when I bumped into something solid.

Something solid that shouldn't be there.

"What in the hell are you doing here with them?" a familiar voice asked from behind me.

I closed my eyes as Dante came out of his office, clearly not happy with the way Wolf's arms were around me.

"Let go of her. Now," Dante ordered, eyes hot.

My eyes widened and I tried to step out of Wolf's embrace, but I couldn't make my feet move.

My body, unlike my mind, liked where it was.

In fact, it liked it so much that I leaned back slightly before realizing just exactly what it was that I was doing.

Then I rocketed forward, waved at Dante and Wolf, and ran out of the room.

I took the stairs that led down to the street at a near run.

The man at my back, however, was twice as fast as me, landing at the bottom in time to catch me before I could go all the way out the door and to freedom.

"Oomph," I hit Wolf's body so hard that I lost my footing and would've gone down to my knees.

Wolf's arms kept me up as he pulled me into his chest and wrapped both arms so tightly around me that I could barely catch my breath.

"What. Are. You. Doing. Here?" he asked, looking down at me with those intense gray eyes of his.

"I'm living," I said stupidly.

His eyes, which were so focused on me that I could see every single striation in his iris, warmed.

"My sister hasn't been able to get a hold of you for weeks now," he said. "Why are you hurting her like that?"

I bit my lip.

How did I tell him that his sister, the woman that had been kidnapped right along with me, brought back bad memories that I was trying to keep buried?

You didn't. You lied.

Which was what I tried to do, but his eyes told me clearly that he didn't believe a word that came out of my mouth.

"I'm really busy," I replied lamely.

"You're really not. Not if you're Travis and Dante's receptionist," he challenged.

My mouth fell open in affront. "Are you telling me that I'm lazy?"

His brows furrowed in confusion. "How, exactly, did you get lazy out of what I said?"

I ran my tongue over my teeth, thinking through what I would say next.

"How's Hannah?" I asked.

"Crushing on some man that she saw," he murmured. "Would you like me to tell her you inquired about her?"

My mouth dropped open.

"You're…you allow her to do that?" I asked.

He blinked.

"I allow her to do whatever she wants. She's a grown ass woman," he replied. "You're stalling."

I was.

Still, he didn't need to have his suspicions confirmed.

Before I could find something else to deter his attention, Dante and Travis appeared on the landing above us.

Travis locked the door as Dante continued down the stairs, his eyes on me. In Wolf's arms.

Why was I still in Wolf's arms?

I pulled away as if he'd burned me, tripping over myself once again so he had to catch me.

Jesus, I was such a klutz.

Dante's eyes narrowed on me, and I had the sinking feeling that he was assessing everything I did, and he didn't like what he was finding out.

Moving away from Wolf once again, I picked up the purse I hadn't realized I'd dropped, pulled the strap over my head, and pushed my way past him towards my car.

I'd just placed my foot onto the smooth concrete right outside when a loud *pop* sounded.

It wasn't a normal sound. It was just a sound. One that didn't affect me in the least.

My eyes swung to the side where I saw Wolf's shiny black bike leaning to one side against the curb, and then to the left to see Dante's white Tahoe, and Travis' black Mustang, only to stop when I saw someone leaning on my car.

"Hey!" I yelled at the man.

Then something tackled me from behind, taking me down so hard that my arm landed funny, raw pain shooting from my fingertips all the way to my shoulder blade.

I cried out in agony, but whomever had hit me wasn't getting up.

In fact, he stayed down so long that I started to panic.

Pop. Pop. Pop.

"Still," Wolf's dark, angry voice growled.

I closed my eyes as silent tears started to slip down my cheeks.

"I think my arm's broken," I moaned, tears clogging my throat and making my words hard to understand.

Wolf understood, though.

Did he get up? No.

He stayed exactly where he was, and when I heard the loud *bang-bang*, I knew why.

The sound of an engine filled my ears and tires squealed in protest as whatever vehicle belonging to those tires sped away.

That's when it finally dawned on me what those first popping sounds I'd heard actually were.

Gunfire.

I was hearing gunfire.

The boys behind me were returning gunfire.

Somebody was shooting at us!

It was long moments after the loud engine disappeared that Wolf finally got up off me, and when he did, the shooting pain intensified so much that I vomited on myself.

"Shit," Wolf growled. "Fuck, I'm sorry."

"Break it?" Travis asked as he hunkered down beside me.

He was reaching behind him, replacing his gun in his holster, I realized.

Dante did the same on my other side while Wolf gently rolled me over.

"Broken as fuck," Dante observed.

My eyes went down, and my head started to whirl as I got a good look at my arm.

It was odd.

Really odd.

I'd never seen my arm that contorted looking before.

That was about the time I passed out.

CHAPTER 3

Muscles will get you to first base. A beard will get you all the way around the bases with my vagina smothering your face right before you slide into home.
-Beardisms

Wolf

My stomach churned as I sat next to Raven on the bed.

Her eyes were on the hot pink cast being placed on her arm as she tried valiantly to do anything but look at me.

I couldn't blame her.

I'd been the one to break her arm after all.

My stomach rolled again, and I closed my eyes, remembering the distinct crack that signaled Raven's arm breaking. *In two fucking places.*

Raven's auburn hair shifted as she turned to look at me, and my eyes locked with hers.

Her almost navy blue irises were so dark that they only brought more attention to her eyes rather than away from them. Compared to her milky white skin, they stood out starkly, making me unable to look away from her gaze.

I tried not to do that anyway, though, seeing as when I did, my mind wandered.

She had a beautiful body, all generous curves and soft skin. She'd be the perfect woman to have underneath you as you took her from behind. Or lying side by side. Then again, on her back would do fine, too, having her padded thighs cradling my hips as I pounded away inside of her.

"I know you didn't mean to," Raven's soft voice broke into my inner turmoil.

I looked up and shrugged.

Didn't matter if I meant to or not. I still had.

The nurse finished up with the casting just as the woman who'd been in a few minutes before to take Raven's payment came in.

"I'm sorry, Ma'am, but your insurance was declined due to non-payment," the woman apologized to Raven as she handed her the insurance card she'd fished out of her pocket earlier.

Raven's face immediately went red.

"Could you give me a moment, please?" Raven asked as she avoided my eyes.

I got up and walked out of the room without answering her, and immediately made my way toward the reception desk that I saw on the way in.

The woman sitting behind the computer was engrossed in a Solitaire game, completely oblivious to me coming up behind her.

"'Scuse me," I rumbled, knowing damn well and good it'd make her jump.

Her whole body did a one eighty in the computer chair, and she looked at me with wide, fear-filled eyes for all of ten seconds before a slow, admiring smile filled her face.

"Can I help you?" she asked, her voice low and husky.

"I want to pay. Where do I do that at?" I moved around her desk, and she followed me with her desk chair.

"I can help you with that," she smiled. "What's your name?"

"I'm paying for my girl." My voice was hard, and I could tell that the mention of 'my girl' didn't sit well with the woman.

"What's her name?" the woman, my eyes went to her name tag, Deena, questioned.

Her fingers hovered over the keyboard, waiting for my next words.

"Raven March. She's in room five with a broken arm," I replied.

Deena's lips thinned as her fingers started to click on the keys of the keyboard.

"I'm showing a four thousand and twenty-dollar bill right now," Deena replied once she'd pulled her name up. "How would you like to pay this? We don't accept checks."

"Don't you have the cash option?" I asked, fishing out my wallet from my back pocket. "If I remember correctly, from the last time I was in here with stitches, it was a flat five hundred dollars."

Deena's mouth went even tighter.

"Yes," she clipped. "Cash or credit card?"

"Cash," I replied, fishing out five one hundred dollar bills from my pocket.

I'd planned to go buy a new pistol today with the money, but plans change, after all, and not always for the better.

It'd all started with the call I'd gotten that morning from one of my informants and had gone straight downhill from there.

I'd intended to talk with Travis, a man that I knew hated my guts, to ask him for help. I had the president of our motorcycle club, Peek set up the meeting. I was going to tag along and hope they would talk to me.

Travis had agreed, but only if Dante could be there, too.

Peek gave his consent to that, knowing damn well and good it was a bad idea, but we had no other options.

I needed the help, and my sister's life depended on it.

I'd do just about anything to keep my sister safe, to stop her suffering, even do something so unpleasant as to meet with the Hail brothers. Peek ended up having a schedule conflict and I had to go to the meet by myself.

"Here's your receipt," Deena handed me a paper, and I took it.

When I returned to the room, Raven was still arguing about her insurance.

"I'm telling you, I paid it this month. I paid it last month. I paid it the month before that. It's current. Please, just try to run it again."

I held my hand up and stopped Raven.

"It's not going to work," I told her.

Both women looked at me, and I handed the receipt over to show I'd paid.

"We're paid up."

The woman took it and read it, nodded once, and then left the room.

"What the hell, Wolf?" Raven asked, steam starting to rise out of the top of her head.

Well, if it were possible it would be.

She was that mad.

I held my hand up and stopped her.

"Let me explain before you go flipping out," I told her.

"Knew I should've listened to Travis and Dante and not come with you," Raven muttered darkly.

My insides clenched at her words.

"I was married to Travis and Dante's sister," I replied softly. "She died when a serial killer, who was targeting cops, shot both of us in the head. She died, I lived, and they blame me."

Raven's eyes went wide at my words.

"Abby?" she asked.

I nodded.

"Abby," I confirmed.

"That's terrible. I'm so sorry for your loss." She touched my arm with her good hand, and her eyes softened.

"Abby and I were having problems. We were on the verge of a divorce, and Abby was pregnant with my child at the time of her death. Dante and Travis blame me, and therefore dislike my club as well. They'd do just about anything to never have to see me again," I informed her. "If I didn't need the help, I would've never shown my face to them. I know it hurts them to see me. But, I have very few options at this point, and my sister's life, as well as yours, now that I realize what is going on, are in danger."

"Why?" Raven asked with confusion. "I haven't done anything."

"Oh, but to him, you have. You testified and put away two of his top producers," I replied.

"Shit," Raven growled. "Why can't I just fucking live my life? I swear, every time I find my footing, something else comes around the corner and knocks me down to my ass again."

I looked over at her and smiled.

"Welcome to the shit club where life is always hard, and you never know what to expect before life knocks you down again," I responded to her outburst.

Raven's smile was forced as she hopped back on the bed, her broken arm cradled to her chest.

"Well, let's go," she said, picking up her things off the bed before she slid back down and started heading to the door.

I grabbed the receipt and followed behind her, nodding to the doctor who'd been taking care of Raven.

He nodded back and I kept pace behind Raven as we made our way out to the front lobby of the ER.

"Hold on," I ordered, stopping her before she could make it to the bank of windows at the very front.

She stopped and turned, looking at me in question.

"What?" she asked.

"Let me check it out before you go out there," I replied, walking ahead of her.

Raven sighed at my back but stayed where she was as I went ahead of her and took a look around.

After seeing nothing remarkable, I walked back inside and gestured her outside with my hand.

She followed, her eyes going to my bike across the parking lot.

"I'm not riding on that," she said.

I looked at her like she was crazy.

"Why not?" I questioned her as I took hold of her good hand and led her to my bike. "Are you scared?"

Her back straightened so fast and hard that I worried for the state of her spine. She didn't resist, and I had to smile as she clutched my hand.

She didn't answer.

It was obvious she didn't like riding. It scared her.

When we rode here, I wasn't sure if she was actually scared of the bike or in pain from the broken arm. Now, I could clearly tell that it was because she feared riding.

"When I was seventeen, I was following behind a motorcycle," she said the moment we reached my bike.

I turned and studied her, wondering where she was going with her line of conversation, but I had a feeling in the back of my mind that what she was about to tell me changed her life.

And not in a positive way.

She was staring at the bike for so long that I wasn't sure she was going to finish, but she shook her head and looked at me before quickly looking away.

"A car pulled out in front of him, and he slammed into the car. Went through the car's windows, and straight into a guardrail that severed him in half at the waist." She shivered at the memory. "He died, all because some woman wasn't paying attention to what she was doing and pulled out in front of him."

"Bikes are less visible on the road, yes," I confirmed. "I've had over twenty-two years of motorcycle riding experience, and I know how to handle my bike. Trust me when I say that, while you're on the back of my bike, no harm will come to you."

She gave me a dry look.

"You can't control the actions of others," she informed me, walking up to the bike and lifting her leg to straddle it.

"I can't," I told her, mounting the bike in front of her. "But if it's within my power to control, I'll make it so."

She hummed and scooted back, giving me some room to move back as well.

When I was comfortable, I started the bike and leaned to the side, kicking the stand up on the bike, before walking it out of the parking spot.

"Do bikes not have reverse?" she yelled over the loud hum of the motor.

I turned until I was facing forward, and then looked at her over my shoulder.

"Most bikes are light enough that the person riding them can push them where they need to be. They also have a tight turning radius, so once it's backed up, even a little bit, we can turn out of the spot," I answered her back, nearly yelling to be heard over the roar of the motor.

She patted my shoulder and I took that as my sign to go, revving the motorcycle's engine and accelerating out of the parking lot.

Luckily, the ride to The Uncertain Saints clubhouse was uneventful, and I pulled into the driveway as far as I could before I had to get off and walk. We could no longer access the house from the parking lot due to the flooding. The boat ramp adjacent to the house was under water also, so we had a makeshift area that we docked our river transportation.

"Whoa," Raven said once the motor died. "How do you get up there?"

I chuckled as I dismounted, holding my hand out to her.

"Boat," I replied. "That one."

I pointed to the one tied to a stake that Peek, the president of The Uncertain Saints MC, and I had pounded into the wet earth. Normally, there were four flat bottom boats tied there, but with three of them gone, and three bikes in the driveway next to mine, it meant that we weren't going to be alone when we got there.

Which was likely good for me.

I didn't need any more distractions than I already had.

The five foot three distraction, with auburn hair and dark blue eyes, was definitely one that would be more of a diversion than most.

"Hop in," I ordered.

She looked at the boat, studied its integrity for a few long moments, and then nodded her head.

"If I die, nobody will care," she mumbled to herself.

I untied the boat and pushed off, the boat scooting across the water toward the stairs on its own volition.

"If I die, somebody will care. They'll look for me and find you," I teased her.

She shot her angry eyes up to mine.

"Shut up."

I grinned down at the water as I picked up the paddle and rowed us to the stairs.

"Grab the railing," I ordered.

She did as directed, grabbed it with her good arm, and immediately climbed out of the boat to the stairs.

In doing so, she lost hold of the boat and I soared past the stairs.

"Shithead," I muttered, rowing back to the stairs.

This time I grabbed the railing and hauled myself up, tying the boat next to all the others that were there before heading up the stairs toward where Raven was waiting.

"I think I should've changed," she muttered, looking down at her pants that were stained with dirt from when I'd pushed her to the ground earlier.

"You're fine," I told her. "At least your clothes don't have blood on them like mine do."

I pointed to the back of my arm where a piece of rock had ricocheted and gouged into the meat right above my elbow, and her eyes widened.

"You've been shot!" she screeched.

So loudly, in fact, that the front door opened and three men filled the doorway, guns in hand.

Raven jumped and flew backwards, going down two steps to crowd behind my back, her cute little face peeking out over my shoulder.

"It's okay, Raven," I patted her hip. "They're not going to hurt you."

"I never said that they were," she muttered.

"Then why are you hiding behind me?" I asked her.

"Ummm," she hesitated, her voice high and unsure. "Because they have guns?"

I snorted.

"That's a pretty darn good read," Casten offered as he replaced his gun in the holster underneath his arm.

I grinned at him and took a hold of Raven's hand, pulling her inside with me.

"Dante and Travis here yet?" I asked them as I walked inside, relief hitting me when I didn't automatically see them staring at me with those cold eyes.

"No," Peek said from behind us as he closed the door. "They haven't made it yet."

"Good," I muttered, dropping Raven's hand and pointing to the kitchen table that was directly across the room from us. "Go take a seat. I'm going to clean this arm up and be right back."

"You can't even reach your arm," Raven countered as she refused to sit. "I'll come help you."

I looked at her, studied her determined face, and then shrugged. "Whatever."

Peek, Mig, Casten and Griffin, my fellow Uncertain Saint members watched us leave with varying degrees of uneasiness following our retreat, and I made a mental note to ask them what crawled up their asses when Raven wasn't in the room.

Something was wrong, and they wouldn't be talking with a stranger in their midst.

"Where's the first-aid kit?" she asked the moment we arrived at the hall bathroom.

She elbowed her way inside, then started to open cabinets without waiting for me to tell her where it was.

"Top shelf, first cabinet," I pointed to the one directly across the room, and she nodded as she hustled toward it.

She pulled it open as I started to unbutton the shirt I was wearing.

Once the last button was undone, I hung my cut up on the back of the bathroom door, then tossed my flannel shirt in the corner of the bathroom by the door before pulling my t-shirt up over my head.

I tossed it on the floor, too, and turned around and held my arm up to get my first good look at the wound.

"Glass," I told her. "There's still some in it. Just a small cut."

"How do you know?" she asked as she pushed up beside me and squinted at the mirror.

I grinned at her and twisted so she could look at the wound itself, instead of the mirror, causing her to moan in pain at the sight of my cut.

"It's not a cut, it's a fucking gunshot wound," she growled.

"No, it's not," I said. "It's likely some sort of ricochet that I received while I was covering you," I informed her.

Dropping down until I could get my elbow under the faucet's water flow, I washed it none too gently with soap and water.

"I'm not sure that's the way it's supposed to be done," she watched me. "You're getting your boobs wet."

"I don't have boobs," I retorted.

She grinned.

"You have pecs. Man breasts," she chattered as she watched me clean my wound.

It was then I realized she was nervous with me.

Whether it was because of the wound I'd sustained, or the fact that she was in a locked, close quarters space was beyond me.

Likely, it was a little bit of both.

I wasn't sure, but I stepped back to give her room anyway, just in case she was feeling trapped.

The moment I stepped backwards, her eyes snapped from her contemplation of the granite countertop to my eyes, then immediately went to work on my arm.

"Turn around," she ordered, twisting her finger around to help me understand what she wanted to do.

I grinned and gave her my back, placing my hand out onto the counter to give her easier access without her having to lean into me.

"It looks like it hurts," she muttered as she poked at it. "Does it hurt?"

I gritted my teeth. "Not at all."

She laughed at me as she pulled out the alcohol as well as the cotton balls.

"Shit," she said. "I just dropped half of them on the ground. Do you think they're okay to pick back up and shove back in the bag?"

I shook my head. "No. Just throw them away. We have more."

Well, not on me, but I knew I could get some if I needed them. I'd seen Peek's wife, Alison, doing her nails the other day and she'd had a bag next to her the size of a white kitchen trash bag.

Apparently, she'd gotten the massive package on sale at a wholesale shop, and she hadn't had to buy cotton balls in the last year and a half since she'd bought it.

"Okay," Raven agreed, not bothering to bend down and pick them up. "This might sting."

My belly tightened at the feel of that cool liquid touching my skin, followed shortly by the burning fire that always shadowed the coolness.

"All done. Do you think a big Band-aid will cover it, or should I use the four by four gauze pads?" she asked.

Then she went on to cover it with the pads without waiting for my reply, and I halfway wondered why she'd even bothered to ask if she wasn't going to wait for my reply.

"Tape," she said, holding her hand out.

I picked up the white tape from the box, then handed it to her over my shoulder.

She took it and ripped a piece off using her teeth.

The act was surprisingly sexy, and I found myself watching her movements as she attended to me.

Her fingers were light on the back of my arm, and my whole body started to sing as I felt her breathing on my shoulder.

Her tongue was caught between her top and bottom teeth, her blue eyes so focused on the task before her that she didn't notice me watching her.

The longer I watched, the more I believed that she'd probably be better off without me.

Raven had gone through some incredibly difficult events in the past year and she'd had a hard life growing up. The poor woman didn't deserve to have all of my fucked up mess in her life. She'd already gone through enough.

With determination in my voice I said, "Are you done yet?"

She nodded, running her finger around the outer edge of the gauze to ensure it stuck.

"Done," she announced. "Are you hurt anywhere else?"

Only my cock, but I doubt you'd be willing to take care of that for me.

Instead of saying that, though, I went with, "No."

She smiled at me and stepped back, immediately bringing her arm to her belly.

"Your arm hurting you?" I asked as I turned around.

"No," she lied.

I rolled my eyes and opened the bathroom door without bothering to dress completely. "Come on. I think we have some community pain pills that we all share."

"Isn't that kind of illegal?" she asked as she followed me closely back through the hallway and out into the main room of the seven-bedroom lake house we called the clubhouse.

All five of the original members of The Uncertain Saints had gone in to buy this place. With each of us donating a hundred thousand dollars, we'd been able to buy prime lakefront property on the beautiful Caddo Lake.

We'd also purchased about fifty acres that surrounded our lake house, giving us the privacy we needed to ensure that no one walked onto our property and witnessed any of our activities. Activities that were sometimes legal, and sometimes not so legal.

"Not illegal," I lied to her. "Each of us has had a script for some at one point in time. Now we have a common area where we keep them in case we need one."

I took her into the kitchen and led her to the Scooby Doo cookie jar that was sitting on the counter, lifted the lid, and reached in for a white pill.

Raven's eyes had widened at seeing that cookie jar filled nearly to the top.

"What the hell?" she breathed. "Why do y'all have that much?"

"Last year, Griffin fractured his hand in an…altercation," Alison said from behind us as she walked to the coffee pot and refilled her cup. "Then, just last month, Peek had his jaw fractured during another altercation." She smiled as she recalled the memory. "And during that same altercation, Mig twisted his knee and it blew up to the size of a watermelon." Alison grinned. "Each time they were prescribed pain meds. When they're done, instead of throwing the bottle out, they get dumped into there. I'd avoid the blue ones, though. Those are a joke."

Raven pulled the cookie jar closer and peered inside.

"Are those little blue pills what I think they are?" Raven asked carefully.

Alison grinned.

I, however, did not.

I'd been on the receiving end of the 'little blue pill joke.' And I hadn't liked it. Not one bit.

My cock hadn't liked it either.

I'd stayed hard for nearly eight hours, and that was the most painful eight hours of my whole existence.

Even when I was shot in the head, it wasn't that bad.

Any other pain, I'd found, was something I could ignore if I had a need to.

A raging erection with no way, nor time, to alleviate it was a major pain in the ass. Especially when you were in court the whole fucking day.

"What happened?" Raven asked, reading my face.

I looked over at Alison whose shoulders were shaking as she filled up her mug, and I glared at her, not bothering to answer.

Mig, the shithead, did.

"Wolf had gotten into a skirmish the night before," Mig said, his eyes lit up in mirth.

I had to laugh at Mig's words. The fight hadn't been a 'skirmish.' It'd been a knockdown, drag-out fight that had nearly ended with me losing half my hand.

Lucky for me, the man I was bringing down had been too drunk to see which end of the ax he'd swung at me.

To protect my face, I'd thrown up my hand in hopes to halt its forward progression toward my face, and found myself with a throbbing hand to show for it.

After subduing the guy, I'd taken him to the sheriff's office, gone to the clubhouse for a quick shower and a few hours of shut eye. The next morning, I had hurriedly grabbed a couple of pills before heading to the courthouse two towns over to testify in a case I'd been a part of.

I'd hurriedly tossed back two pain pills, but what I hadn't realized was that as a joke, one of the members had put a bottle of Viagra—an erection inducing pill that helped you stay hard for hours—into the cookie jar.

I'd swallowed a pill along with my pain pill, not realizing what I'd taken until later that morning.

"And while he was in court the whole day, he had a raging erection that wouldn't go down for nothin'," Mig continued with the story.

My grimace didn't even stop him from telling it all, all the way down to the very nitty gritty.

"So he's sitting on the stand, sweating fucking buckets, and he's dying of blue balls," Mig persists. "We all wondered what the hell was going on, but never figured it out until later that night when he comes in, hot as a hornet, and walks straight to the cookie jar and finds those in it."

Raven burst out laughing, her eyes filled with happiness as she turned to me.

"That's...funny," she grins. "I'm sorry."

"It was funny. But he's never let us forget what happened to him," Mig supplies. "Fucking hilarious, but he's gotten us all back a time or two now."

"How?" Raven asks, her eyes wide.

Mig grimaces.

"There are a lot of pills that look like that white one in your hand," Mig gestures to the pill that Raven had yet to take.

Raven's eyes went wide, and she looked at the pill like it was some mutant that was about to kill her.

"It's the right one," I told her. "The pill has those markings right there."

I indicated the letters in the pill, and her whole body sagged with relief.

"Good," she whispered, searching the room for something.

"Drink?" I questioned.

She nodded, and I walked to the fridge.

Pulling out a Coke and a water, I held them both up to her.

"Which one?" I asked.

She pointed to the water, and I put the Coke back before handing the water over.

She took the pill and downed half the water.

I looked at her in surprise.

"That's impressive," I said.

"Would be more impressive if she could do that with a beer and not water," Mig offered as he left the room.

Raven giggled, and I took another step away from her.

Giggling wasn't normally something that did it for me, but those cute sounds coming out of that mouth made my deflating dick start to harden once again.

She frowned at my sudden departure, but I turned my back on her and walked out of the kitchen, straight to the living room window that overlooked the lake.

The clubhouse was an open concept house. The kitchen flowed into the living room and dining room. It appeared to be one large room, and each side of the large area had doors that led to hallways. The hallways led to the bedrooms that flanked each side of the house. Four on one side, and three on the other.

One of those rooms we used as our meeting room, or 'church' as some of us liked to call it.

My eyes took in the river that swelled over its usual banks, coming to just a few feet from the balcony instead of where it typically stopped, about fifteen feet from the balcony.

Caddo Lake was beautiful anytime, but in early spring when the trees had the fresh green leaves of new life was my favorite.

The water being up so high didn't take away from the natural beauty of the lake, but instead enhanced it.

My eyes went to a boat that I'd seen passing by when we'd arrived earlier, and I narrowed my eyes on them.

It was a flat bottom boat similar to the ones we were using to carry us from the end of the driveway to the clubhouse, but this one had a shiny little motor on the back that was way too big for such a small vessel.

My anger grew as I saw the kids doing donuts in the boat, circling it around so fast that the wake started to wash up onto the back deck, coming perilously close to the back door.

Gritting my teeth, I walked outside, ignoring the way the water rushed up against my feet, and walked to the balcony.

Lifting my fingers to my lips, I whistled sharply, causing the boys to look up and stop what they were doing.

Knowing what would work best, I reached into my back pocket where I'd stashed my badge, and held it up high for them to see.

The boys froze, and each looked at the other before waving in understanding.

Hooking the badge to my belt, I crossed my arms over my chest and stared at them until they understood.

They rode off, but this time they were mindful of the 'no wake zone' that the entire fucking river had been designated.

Thinking they needed a little more scare in their blood, I withdrew my phone from my pocket and quickly tapped out Core's number.

Core was our newest member, and also a game warden that patrolled our area.

Knowing he'd be close, I hit send and waited for him to answer.

"Yeah?" Core answered.

"Where are you?" I asked without a greeting.

"About two minutes up the lake at the only boat ramp left. Why?" he asked, sounding distracted.

Perfect.

"There's about to be a fourteen-foot flat bottom making its way to you. They're not heeding the no wake zone," I informed him.

"Dammit. Nobody is. I'm going to have to get out there and inform them of their blatant disregard for the rules and probably ticket them for it," Core growled.

Core, not one to be moody even at the worst of times, sounded downright pissed off.

I wondered if his day had been as bad as mine but chose not to question him right now.

During my phone call, Raven had made her way out to the porch and was now leaning on the railing beside me, her eyes taking in the lake before us.

"Well, you can start with those two," I told him.

"Got it. Later," Core hung up and I stuffed my phone back into my pocket.

"Your skin is kind of tanned for it being only April," Raven observed from my side.

I turned my head down to look at her, then shrugged.

"Mow without a shirt on," I informed her. "And my mother is half-Hispanic."

She lifted her head in understanding.

"Got it," she said. "Dante and Travis are here. A big, older man told me to tell you."

I nodded my head and turned back for the door, opening it and holding it open for Raven to pass through.

"Take a seat on the couch. You look like you're about to fall over," I ordered.

She gave me a weak smile. "Pain meds knock me out. If y'all don't hurry, I'll be snoring away on the couch while y'all are talking."

I lifted my head in understanding, then looked up to find Alison.

"Can you get her some coffee?" I asked. "I need her coherent for what I'm telling them."

Alison nodded from her perch against the kitchen counter and turned to get a coffee cup down from the cabinet above her head.

"How do you take it, sweetie?" Alison asked.

I took that as my cue to head to my room at the very back of the left hallway.

I headed straight for the dresser where I kept clean shirts and pants, as well as a few valuables that I might need.

My place was about forty-five minutes away from this one, and pretty inconvenient to hit up when I was in need of something.

Hence, why I was usually here on the days that Nathan stayed with his grandma.

Which was what he was doing tonight, thank God.

My head was not in the right place, and after the day I'd just had, I needed to be careful.

Once I was fully dressed, I walked back out into the kitchen to find Raven sandwiched in between Travis and Dante, who looked none too happy about being here.

"Well, now that you've finally decided to grace us with your presence, how about you get started so we can leave. This place is making it hard to breathe," Travis growled.

I looked at him, studied the tightness around his mouth, and nodded.

"I came to you to ask if you could find whomever is trying to steal my identity; but I can now see that it's not going to work," I replied. "I have other contacts."

Dante's mouth tightened, and Travis' eyebrows shot up.

"You came to ask me for a favor?" he blurted.

Travis was a good man. He never told someone in need no…unless it was me. Then he had absolutely no problem saying no.

"Yes," I replied. "But I've already called in other favors, so I'll no longer be needing your help. Raven, however, does need your help. If what I suspect is true, whomever is doing this is targeting everyone that was involved in my sister's kidnapping, including Raven."

Travis sighed, opened his mouth, but Raven beat him to it.

"You think someone's trying to steal my identity?" she asked.

I shrugged.

"At this point, I'm not real sure of anything, I just have some suspicions," I responded. "Four days ago I tried using my bank card and got denied. An hour after that, I called and heard that my accounts had been frozen due to fraudulent activity." I walked to the coffee pot and poured myself a drink, nodding at Alison's sympathetic gaze before turning back to Dante and Travis who were now turned around in their seats and facing me. "Lucky for me, I still had my account under Abby's name, and they didn't find all of my information. That changed a day later, but I'd already moved all of my money to a different account under a different name."

Travis kept staring, so I continued.

"My car insurance was canceled along with my driver's license, health insurance, and my fucking storage facility. Everything credit-wise that I had in my name was compromised," I explained.

"What about your house...your bike?" Travis asked, his attention caught.

"Paid for. No bank loans," I answered.

"What makes you think Raven's in the same boat?" Travis asked. "It could be isolated to just you."

I shook my head.

"Her insurance was declined today," I informed them.

"That shouldn't be. We pay her insurance," Dante murmured, adding his input now.

I nodded my head. "I know."

"What else do you have?" Dante countered.

"Credit card bills being opened in my name. Checks being written all over town. My water company called and asked if I was sure I wanted to cancel service," I persisted. "Everything that has my name attached to it is being affected."

"You've looked into it?" he asked.

"Yes," I nodded. "My sister's having much of the same problem. Her husband is a firefighter, who's not being affected. Yet. Luckily, most of the things in my sister's name are already paid for."

"Do you have any leads?" Dante asked.

"Not at first, no." I relied. "Last week, though, my sister said she was having some trouble with her credit card. So I started to get suspicious." I took a sip of my coffee, then set it down by my left elbow. "Not everybody in the entire MC was starting to have the similar problems with their credit so I started trying to figure out why just certain brothers were involved. The only ones who helped me in the case of my sister's kidnapping, who were mentioned in the police report, were Griffin, Mig and Casten. Pairing that with my sister and her husband, and now hearing that Raven's insurance isn't working starts to confirm my suspicions. That was how my sister's started."

Travis' eyes went narrow as I spoke.

"I can run a few searches when I get home," Travis muttered.

Raven's eyes went from me to Travis, her eyes wide and surprised. "You told me you don't like computers."

"That's 'cause Trav likes to break into places he's not allowed to. If he can't do what he wants, he doesn't do it at all," Dante said absently. "Anything besides the identities?"

"Not yet," I muttered, picking my coffee back up.

And I did mean that. It hadn't happened…yet. But it would. This was only the beginning.

The beginning that hopefully was caught before it could get too out of control.

CHAPTER 4

Forgive and forget. Fuck that and fuck you, fucking fucker.
-Raven's secret thoughts

Raven

"I'll take care of your accounts as soon as I get home," Travis climbed up the steps ahead of me.

"Thank you," I replied to his back, snorting when he kept walking without looking back.

I should've known that would be how he reacted.

The man loved a challenge, and that'd been something I'd witnessed a lot over the last few months since I'd been working with him.

I was still amused to know that he actually liked computers. I thought that he disliked them due to his inability to use one with those fat fingers of his. To my surprise, he was not only comfortable working with the computer, but he was actually good at it.

Opening my door with the wrong hand proved to be a challenge, but it worked out well enough.

"No!" I yelled. "Don't jump!"

My dog, a white German Shepherd that I'd somehow become the proud new owner of the week before I'd left, jumped anyway, but not on my body.

She jumped in front of the door to ensure that I couldn't open it.

The door threw open with a slam, and I sighed.

"That was almost my fingers, you big beast," I growled, walking past him to the couch that was directly in line with the front door.

The TV, which I know for a fact I didn't leave on, was blaring, and I turned another glare on Marky Mark.

Marky Mark looked at me with those big brown eyes of his, jaw hanging open wide, and tongue lolling.

Marky Mark wasn't his real name. When I came home and found him in my yard, no one was laying claim to him. It was the week before I was to leave Kilgore, so with no other recourse, I decided to keep him, and I renamed him. He didn't respond to it at first, but eventually he came around.

Marky Mark hadn't been the original name that I'd used, but then I'd gotten home the first time, after deciding to keep him, and found the TV blaring with Marky Mark playing on an old show on MTV.

After teasing him about being a Marky Mark fan, I'd decided to use that as his name.

He seemed accepting enough, and that had been that.

He didn't like it quiet while he was home alone, and it took a smart dog to turn the TV on by himself, but he managed it.

I no longer worried about how it'd gotten on.

After it happened in the middle of the night a few weeks ago, I'd gotten up and turned it off, only for it to turn on again not two minutes later.

After turning it off a second time, I'd caught Marky Mark pressing his wet nose to the button on the front of the TV, and realized that it was my dog doing it—not some psycho who liked to see me scared out of my mind.

"Seriously, though." I shook the TV changer at him. "All you have to do is turn it on. You don't have to turn it up so high that the neighbors hear it!"

When he didn't respond or even blink and act like he acknowledged me, I tossed the TV changer onto the couch and walked to the kitchen.

Immediately upon arriving, I opened the puke green fridge that I'd found at a garage sale and reached inside for an adult beverage.

AKA a Mountain Dew. My weakness.

A weakness that I hadn't had before being kidnapped.

During our captivity, we'd only been served tea. And not even good tea at that.

The moment I'd gotten saved—by Wolf—I'd asked for something to drink.

The only thing Wolf had was a Mountain Dew. It'd been so good—so fucking perfect—that I drank them just to remind myself that I was alive.

This time I drank it with a pain killer I'd stolen from the communal cookie jar at the Uncertain Saints' clubhouse just before I'd left.

Tomorrow, I'd go fill my prescriptions, but until then this would work just fine.

I'd just swallowed my first pill when I decided that maybe I should've eaten like my doctor, as well as Wolf, had instructed me to.

The moment I looked into the fridge, though, I realized how futile that endeavor was.

There was no food in my fridge. There was also no food in my cupboards.

I'd not gone to the store in at least three weeks, and I'd been surviving on Ramen noodles and tuna fish.

Tonight, neither of those would be sufficient.

A: Because I didn't have any of the two aforementioned things. B: Because I was tired of them, even if I did have them.

With nothing left to do but go to the store, I darted into my room and changed out of my dirty shorts.

The first thing I found to change into were the jeans I'd bought at Goodwill my senior year in college.

They still fit, but they were definitely on the verge of being too tight.

They were thin and comfortable, but I had to jump and twist to get them onto my body.

Once they were on, though, they felt like butter.

They fit me like a second skin, and I knew they made my ass look fantastic.

An ass that was on the side of leaning towards too big.

Once I slipped my feet into my shoes, once again, I headed to the living room and picked up my car keys. Once they were in my hand, I whistled to Marky Mark and picked up my purse.

"Wanna go for a ride?" I asked him.

Not having to be asked twice whether he wanted to go for a ride or not, he launched himself off my couch and skidded to a stop in front of the door.

Marky Mark was in love with the car. His favorite pastime was riding with the window down and half his body stuck out of it.

I'd actually been scared shitless the first few times he'd done it, but the more I became used to his ways, and the more he showed me that he could obviously handle having the front half of his body hanging out, the less I worried.

The trip down the stairs was just as painful going down as it was going up, and I was panting with the effort it took to hold my arm still once I reached the bottom of the stairs.

The apartment I lived in was actually a neighboring apartment to the one that Travis lived in when I first moved here.

It was at the top of the garage that housed all the vehicles that Hail Auto Recovery used for their business. Although not at the same time. Mostly, this garage was used for storage of the extra vehicles, as well as doing any maintenance on the wreckers that needed to be done—scheduled or unscheduled. They had ten wreckers that they used on a regular basis, and at any given time, a few were in the shop for some reason or another.

Mostly, though, the men—and one woman—who drove the wreckers kept them with them due to the afterhours callouts that came in. There was a central office in the garage as well that two dispatchers manned. One was seven to three, and the other was three to eleven. During the day, Travis, Dante, or I helped man the phones.

Dante and Travis no longer drove the wreckers, having graduated from doing that once they reached their five truck mark.

Descending the steps, I had my head down, one hand in my purse searching for my keys, and the other on the railing as I moved quickly.

I'd just hit the bottom step when I hit something solid causing my head to jerk back and my eyes to widen.

"Shit!" I hissed, nearly falling backwards.

The strong hand that caught me before I fell, though, was startling to say the least.

The angry black eyes belonging to Wolf were nothing less than breathtaking.

"You scared the hell out of me," I gasped, my hand going over my heart as if I could control the beating by doing so.

Wolf glared. "What are you doing outside all by yourself?"

"Groceries," I replied shortly, my teeth worrying my lip.

"Groceries," he repeated, sounding incredulous.

I nodded.

"You're lucky it was me and not someone else. Fancy a few bullet holes in your body?" Wolf asked almost casually.

I let go of my lip with my teeth and glared at him.

"What are you talking about?"

"You're supposed to be with someone if you absolutely have to leave. Didn't you pick up on this sometime earlier this afternoon? You know, when someone was shooting at us?" Wolf growled.

"Nobody told me I needed to fucking hide! Nor did I ever hear that I needed an escort if I left my house!" I yelled, waving my arms wildly.

Wolf's emotions were volatile, and I was not only surprised at the rage he felt at me leaving my apartment unattended, but I was also flabbergasted that he cared that much.

I was just a nobody. I was seriously only a girl that he saved, not because I'd been the one he'd come for, but because I'd been the one there when the one he did come for was rescued.

I was a mess and a half, and people like me didn't get worried about by people like Wolf.

"I figured the fucking bullets being shot at us earlier, as well as the fact that Travis escorted you home, were enough to make that logical leap," Wolf replied sarcastically.

I gritted my teeth, and only just refrained from fisting my hand.

"Just for your information, Travis always takes me home. How was I supposed to know that I should be watching what I was doing?" I asked him. "And I thought the bullets were because of you! Not me! If I'd known that they were meant for me as well, I sure as fuck wouldn't be walking around after dark."

Wolf's eyes went down to my dog, and then back up to me.

"Nice dog," he said.

I looked down at Marky Mark, then back up to his black eyes.

"He's a good boy," I agreed. "Now, what are you doing here?"

"Taking you to get groceries, I guess," Wolf muttered darkly.

I gave him an ugly look, causing his mouth to twitch in response.

"What are you doing here, really?" I asked.

"Meeting with Travis." He didn't expound on his answer, and I had to grit my teeth in order to control the urge to shout at him.

That, or knee him in the nuts.

Not that I would ever, ever do that. The thought might cross my mind occasionally, but I would have to wager a bet that the moment my knee made contact it wouldn't take him down.

Yes, it'd hurt him.

Would it stop him, though?

Hell to the no.

He'd probably get super powers by me doing that to him. Superpowers that made it possible to wring my neck with only a glance.

"Thanks for offering that titillating information," I growled.

Wolf's mask slipped, and I saw him smile for the fourth time in all the months that I'd known him.

"Titillating?" he parroted.

I sighed.

"We'll have to take my car, because I don't think you can fit the amount of groceries I need into those tiny little saddle bags," I informed him.

He grinned.

"Got the truck today, dear," he said tonelessly. "Come on."

He led me to a dark brown Chevy, a fully restored one that dated back to before I was born. I couldn't tell you a date. What I could tell you was that it was beautiful, and it looked like he put a lot of effort into it.

I'd seen it before, of course, but never out of the garage that Wolf housed it in.

Both times that I noticed it at July's house, she told me that he didn't drive it very often.

Apparently, it was something he'd put a lot of time and effort into building, and he didn't drive it because, according to him, 'people were stupid and didn't know how to drive.'

Which begged me to question why was he driving it now?

Ignoring my need to question him, I walked up to the truck and headed to the passenger side, only to have Wolf stop me and usher me to the driver's side.

"Car seat," he explained.

I blinked.

"You'll have to sit in the middle," he told me as he opened the door.

I blinked.

"Ummm," I hesitated. "We can take my car. I have a backseat and no car seats at all."

Not to mention more space, meaning I wouldn't have to touch him or be close to him.

There was no telling what my crazy self would do if I was that close to him.

He smelled divine already. Being in an enclosed space with him only inches away was likely going to kill me.

He ignored my offer, though, and gave me a slight push in the middle of my back to urge me inside.

I went, but only because I was still recovering from the fact that he'd touched me.

He'd never done that before.

Oh, my God!

I felt like I had a searing handprint in the middle of my back, right over my bra strap, burning through every layer of my clothing and melting straight into my bones.

Crawling in and scooting all the way over as far as the car seat on the bench seat would allow me, I came to a stop and crossed my arms over my chest.

"Seatbelt," he ordered from where he was standing outside the truck, his eyes directed downwards at my dog who was sitting next to him instead of crawling inside with me.

Once I was inside, he led Marky Mark around to the passenger side and pointed to the floor board.

Marky Mark went willingly, and then curled into a tight ball underneath the dash.

Wolf slammed the door closed and rounded the hood, rendering me momentarily dysfunctional as I watched his tight body move under the light of the street lamp.

When he took his place beside me, I snapped to attention and started scrambling.

I reached between us, accidentally scraping the back of my hand down his thigh in my search for the belt.

When I couldn't find it, I turned in my seat slightly, giving him my back, as I looked for it.

"Might be behind the seat," he muttered, reaching behind my back, right where my ass was, and snaked his hand into the crack of the seat searching for the elusive seatbelt.

His big body pinned mine in, ensuring that I had nowhere to go while he pressed his luscious chest to my back.

"Damn, it's hung," he said, leaning forward even more.

This time his hips were pressed to my back, and I froze at the very sizeable cock that was poking me in the back.

The scary thing, though, was that I didn't think he was hard.

It didn't feel like it. It was definitely a cock, though.

There was no hiding the way it was positioned in his pants, nor the way it felt against my backside.

Something clicked and clanked, and suddenly all that heavenly body heat was gone from my back as he pulled the seatbelt free of the seat.

"Here," he said, placing it over my lap.

I reached for it and our hands brushed, causing my face to flame.

"Scoot closer to me, or widen your legs," Wolf ordered.

I looked up at him in confusion.

"What?" I asked.

He started the truck, and then wiggled the stick that was somehow magically between my legs.

"Would be easier for you to part them, but you can do whatever's more comfortable for you," he moved the stick again.

It was then I realized that the truck was a five speed, and the fucking shifter was between my freakin' legs!

Meaning his hand had to reach over my thigh to get to it—if I parted my legs.

If I didn't part my legs and scooted closer to him, not only would that make me practically on top of him, but that would also cause him to have to reach over both of my legs to get to the shifter. Making his hand rest practically in my lap.

I chose to part my legs.

It seemed the lesser of two evils.

At first it was smooth rolling.

I was in my seat, my legs parted, and we were driving out of the parking lot.

Then he shifted gears.

First wasn't too bad. Second not bad either.

Third was the best because that meant his arm was about as far away from my leg as he could get in the truck cab.

Fourth, however, was not good.

Fourth was down and directly in the middle of my legs.

And when I say middle, I mean in the middle.

Right up against my crotch.

Without me there, it was very obvious that the shifter nearly touched the seat.

With his hand on the shifter and in fourth gear, it meant that his fingers not only overlapped the seat, but they were fucking touching me.

In my crotch.

At first I didn't think he realized it.

I sure as hell did, though.

In fact, I was practically hyperventilating.

His knuckles were skimming the seam of my jeans. The same seam that was pressed up tightly against my clit since they were so tight.

Oh, God. I closed my eyes. *What the hell was I thinking wearing these jeans out of the house instead of cleaning in them like I usually did?*

Thankfully—for once in my life—I was happy that someone pulled out in front of me, meaning Wolf down shifted and removed his hand from my vagina's usual stomping grounds.

Just as quickly as that thought appeared, it fled.

He wasted no time accelerating back up to speed, and it was obvious after a full minute of having his hand pressed up against my crotch that he didn't intend to go any faster than he was at that very moment.

"So," I said, feeling the need to make small talk. "How's Nathan?"

His mouth quirked as a smile appeared on his face.

"He's with his grandma," he replied. "He's spending about half the time at her place, and half the time at mine. With me working as much as I do, we thought it best that she take him Monday through Thursday, and I take him Friday through the weekend. If I'm not busy, I have him during the week as well. It all just depends on my schedule."

"Is this your mother?" I continued with the line of questioning, my eyes nearly crossing when he repositioned his hand on the gear shift.

"No. This is his father's mother," he replied.

My brows furrowed.

"What?" I asked in confusion.

Wolf smiled sadly.

"Nathan's adopted. His real father was my best friend, and was killed along with Nathan's mother," he said.

I turned my head to study Wolf.

His face was carefully blank, and each streetlight we passed lit his face enough that I could tell that this subject was not something he wanted to talk about, so like the wise woman I was, I changed the subject.

"How am I supposed to live my life if I have to be watched twenty-four seven?" I asked him.

He turned to look at me for a few long seconds before his eyes went back to the road in front of him.

"What I was expecting was for you to go to work with Travis, and for Travis to take you home after y'all were done for the day," he replied. "Why are you working for them anyway?"

He turned into the parking lot that sported a supermarket, Dollar General, and Waffle House –three of the only things that the tiny stretch of highway had to offer, and parked the truck.

Thankful that I no longer had Wolf's hand within my vaginal boundaries, I scooted out.

"Stay," I ordered Marky Mark when he went to follow me.

"He can come inside," Wolf said absently as he scanned his surroundings, his dark eyes on the dark area at the back of the parking lot.

I took the chance to study him.

Wolf was a big man, and when I say big, I mean he's bigger than anyone I've ever met.

I've met some large men in my life, but Wolf definitely topped the charts.

He had a tall, muscular build that drew the eyes to the tops of his shoulders as well as his hard, thick thighs that were encased in light washed jeans.

He had on his Uncertain Saints MC cut that was black with red lettering and accents.

The black angel wings on the back looked freakin' awesome as well, making me want to laugh.

Wolf was anything but an angel, that was for sure.

His body was made for debauchery, and those dark eyes, paired with his black hair and deeply tanned skin screamed sinner for sure.

That ass in those jeans, though.

Jesus Christ, was it lovely.

"Ready?" he asked, bringing my attention from the state of his ass to his face, which was looking straight at me and no longer across the parking lot.

Those dark eyes of his were filled with laughter, and I nearly passed out from embarrassment.

My face flamed.

Shit!

Lani Lynn Vale

CHAPTER 5

You look like I need a drink. Or a blow job. Either one will be good, just as long as both don't include you.
-T-shirt

Wolf

"Ready?" I asked, looking over my shoulder at Raven.

Raven's eyes snapped from my ass to my face, and she blushed a lovely shade of crimson that glowed pink in the harsh light that shone above our heads. In fact, it was so pink that I would almost say it matched the pink cast that was on her wrist.

"Yes," she said, holding her hand out for her dog.

I looked down at the beautiful white German Shepherd, smiled inwardly, and returned my gaze to the stunning sight before me.

Goddamn, was she wearing tight jeans.

I could practically make out every line of her curves in those jeans stretched over.

Although she was short, it definitely did not make her any less sexy.

I didn't normally go for the short girls.

I was a tall guy.

I was also rough around the edges and definitely wasn't one to handle breakable things with care.

Raven was definitely breakable.

Her hands were tiny, something that I realized moments later when I took one of them into my own and pulled her along in my wake when she refused to look at me after I caught her checking out my ass.

Marky Mark—a name so ridiculous that I couldn't even bring myself to say it aloud—followed on Raven's other side, staying close enough to her that he could protect her if she was in need, but also far enough away so he wouldn't be a hindrance if she needed to get away.

Something that he appeared to be trained to do.

"Wonder what happened there," Raven asked, pointing at the store's front door.

"Someone tried to drive their car through the glass," the young girl, all of eighteen, said from behind the checkout counter.

I blinked, taking another look at the boarded up window, and saw the damage that was concealed by the racks of clothes on the outside, and the rack of Cheetos on the inside.

"Damn," I said. "Was the guy drunk?"

The girl shook her head and pulled her phone out of her apron pocket.

"No. The lady had a gunshot wound or something to her chest and her foot jammed on the gas. Her son, who's only seven, saved her life and ours. She almost hit us." She showed the photo to me, turning her phone around without giving it up.

"Damn," I repeated. "That's impressive."

The girl nodded and clicked the button that shut her phone's screen off before shoving it back into her apron.

"It was. Kid deserves a gold medal or something."

I, on the other hand, wondered why the hell she had a gunshot wound.

The picture she showed me didn't have any bullet holes in the car, which meant that whatever had happened, had happened before she got into the car.

My mind went back to earlier as it tried to connect the dots, but whatever link I thought I could match up was gone the moment Raven's hand brushed my dick.

It might've been accidentally, but she did it nonetheless.

"I'm sorry," she rushed out as she steered the cart away from me.

I grunted in reply, trying to calm myself and my dick.

My dick, however, didn't care that it was an accident. All it cared about was the fact that she'd touched it.

With her hand.

Her soft, small hand that would make my dick look massive if it was wrapped around it.

And her hand was so white, that it would stand out starkly against my bronzed skin.

Just the sight of her hand trying to make it around the girth…

"Well, are you coming or what?" Raven interrupted my fantasy.

I sighed.

"Yeah, yeah," I replied, picking up my speed until I was directly behind her.

The crest of her ponytail, which was on the very top of her head, came up to my collarbone. I could see everything over her head, even the attention she drew from the men buying beer across the store.

"You know them?" I asked her, coming up to her side and glaring at the two of them.

They were both young, likely around Raven's age of twenty-seven or so.

Both were quite good looking, but it was more than obvious that they didn't have what it took to capture Raven's attention, especially if the look she gave them before returning her gaze to me was anything to go by.

"They're a couple of the tow truck drivers," she replied. "Billy and...Matt? Mark? Mills? Hell, I can't remember."

I wanted to laugh, but I didn't dare. She'd likely think I was laughing at her, and I most certainly didn't want to piss her off.

I was still trying to decide what this feeling in my chest whenever she was around or I thought about her was.

It'd been there for months and hadn't lessened in the time since she'd left. The moment I saw her today, though, it'd gotten stronger.

Became *deeper.*

"What do you need to get?" I asked her as we started into the produce aisle.

The store was set up in sections. When you walked in the door, the traffic flow was directed to the right and dumped directly into the produce section.

Raven obviously didn't go for veggies, seeing as she'd sped right past them and straight into the cold section.

The first thing she grabbed was a gallon of chocolate milk, followed by three packages of those break-and-bake cookies, one package of canned biscuits, four packages of cheese and twelve Lunchables.

"You know this shit is filled with harmful ingredients like MSG, right?" I asked her, eyeing the processed cheese she threw into the cart with barely contained disgust.

"I don't like to cook," she said. "In fact, I would say I hate to cook. I suck at it. Hence the shit I don't have to actually cook in order to eat."

"Hmm," I hummed. "You know, I could teach you how to cook. Travis is an excellent cook as well. Dante's wife isn't half bad, either."

She ignored the offers and instead focused on an endcap that had marshmallows shaped like dinosaurs. Picking them up, she tossed them in the cart before replying.

"I'm not kidding. I can burn water. And toast. I've been known to occasionally burn my Pop-Tarts," she said as she turned away from the cold section and directed her cart down the canned spaghetti aisle.

She stopped in front of the canned soups and picked up one that claimed to be 'Beer and Cheese.'

"That looks...gross." I chose the word carefully, specifically steering my vocabulary away from anything that might come off as sounding like it was vomit inducing.

The next thirty minutes went like this: she picked up unhealthy foods, I commented about their unhealthiness, and she put them into the cart anyway. It continued like that until she reached the end and moved to the check-out.

I grabbed a granola bar made of whole grain oats and nearly ran into her when she turned abruptly.

"Stay here," she ordered. "Keep my place in line. I'm going to go grab some beer."

I stayed, but made sure to keep her in my line of sight as I watched her move to the far wall and open the glass doors that held the beer.

Picking up a case of the cheapest beer ever made, she carried it awkwardly to where she'd parked her nearly overflowing cart.

Once she was close enough, I grabbed the case of beer from her and set it on the conveyor belt before walking up to the cashier and paying for my granola bar.

Once I had my change, I stood off to the side and let the grocery sacker, a young man about sixteen or seventeen, stuff the plastic bags so full that I was worried they'd break the moment I started carrying them up Raven's stairs.

I didn't say anything and nearly laughed when Raven pushed the boy away from her bags.

"Cold goes with cold," she explained. "Boxes with boxes. Cans with cans. You don't intermix them, and you certainly don't put the bread in with fucking cans."

The boy's face reddened, and I saw them narrow.

"Don't even think about it," I murmured to the kid softly. "You won't win this."

He snapped his mouth shut on whatever rude thing he was about to say and then walked away without a backwards glance.

The checker who showed me the picture earlier on her phone started snickering. "You wouldn't believe how many people have told him that already. I think he does it on purpose now. You have a very well behaved dog."

I looked down at Raven's dog, MM, and nodded. He was well behaved. Marky Mark looked to be a highly trained guard dog. Whoever lost him must have spent a lot of money on his training.

Without another word, we were walking out to the truck while Raven studied her receipt.

"I think they overcharged me for my pickles," she muttered.

"Go back inside and tell them," I suggested.

She shook her head.

"No," she replied. "It's just a dollar."

I rolled my eyes and refrained from saying, 'Then why'd you say anything about it at all?'

Wisely, I kept silent and loaded bags into to the truck's bed, my mind thinking back to the one time, and only time ever, I'd questioned my wife about something very similar to what Raven had just commented on.

It'd been about a year into our marriage, and I'd gone with Abby to the grocery store, much the same way I'd just done with Raven.

We'd bought fifteen million cans of condensed soup and, on one single can out of the fifteen million we'd gotten, they'd charged us an extra dollar for.

We'd spent a total of fifty-two dollars and forty-eight cents, and Abby had been livid.

She'd wanted me to go inside and show them my badge and force them to give me my dollar back.

I, on the other hand, had thought that was ridiculous and had loaded the bags in the truck, much like I'd just done, and ordered her into the truck.

She didn't speak to me for a week for that one.

It'd only gotten worse over the three years we'd been married, and I'd learned to leave it fucking be.

In a last-ditch effort to save our marriage, I, being the dumbass that I was, got her pregnant.

That had not gone over well.

She'd been pissed about that as well, and although she carried the baby we made—one of the rare occasions that she actually gave me her pussy—she hated me. She wanted a divorce, and by the time I realized I wanted it to, we'd found out that we couldn't divorce.

Not until Abby was no longer pregnant. Apparently, in the great state of Texas, if a woman is pregnant, she and her husband cannot divorce until after the child is born.

"What are you doing out there, catching flies?" Raven yelled from the cab.

I snapped my mouth shut and loaded the last bag into the back before I returned the cart to the buggy return.

My eyes caught on some movement at the back of the lot, and I nodded my head at the shadow.

The 'shadow' in question was Mig, a man who was a member of the Uncertain Saints with me.

He was doing some investigating tonight, hoping to catch the person who tried to shoot a few holes in us earlier. It was, of course, a long shot, but we were willing to try anything at this point.

Mig was one of the Saints members who was also a victim of the same identity theft attack that I was and he wasn't very happy about it.

Mig was a wealthy man and owned quite a bit of stock in Konn Vodka, his father's company. Although he had safeguards in place, he wasn't exactly thrilled that he'd had to hire extra people to cover him in case anything got past his safeguards.

Mig was more of a proactive member of the Uncertain Saints rather than a sit back and wait kind of guy.

"Heeellllooooooo," Raven sang from the front seat. "I kinda have to pee, and you're taking forever."

Giving a final nod to Mig, I walked to the driver's side of the truck and dropped inside.

The moment my ass hit the seat, the smell of Raven filled my lungs.

I started to breathe in deeply, and she started to laugh.

"What are you doing?" she asked.

"Nothing," I muttered. "Buckle up."

She rolled her eyes but did it without question, placing her legs together this time forcing me to sit extra close to her.

However, before we'd even left the parking lot, I realized it wasn't going to work.

"I need to get it into fourth, and it's not going to happen with your legs right there. You're gonna have to spread 'em," I informed her, patting her leg for emphasis.

She growled low in her throat, and I had to hide my smile to keep her from taking my head off.

"Fine," she said, spreading her legs, her left leg pressed against mine on one side of the shifter, and her right leg on the other side of the shifter with her foot sharing the floorboard of the passenger side with Marky Mark. "Should've taken my car."

"Your car is too small for my big ass," I told her. "I'd be hitting my head on the roof of the car."

"Travis has no problem getting in," she offered.

I shrugged. "Travis is also about seven inches shorter than my six foot three," I pointed out.

She stuck her tongue out at me.

The move, so innocent, set my blood on fire.

I gritted my teeth and faced forward, my eyes working ahead of me and behind me, but making a point of it to not to look at her again all the way back to her place.

She, of course, had no fucking clue what she was doing to me.

I nearly moaned when I shifted down into third.

Although, the first time I actually brushed against her when I'd shifted into third on our ride there, she'd jumped like a scalded cat.

This time, though, I got nothing more than a shiver.

A delicious, full-body shiver that had my eyes drawing to her perky breasts encased in that tight t-shirt that stretched like a second skin across her chest.

She chattered along about this and that trying to hide her nervousness until we arrived in her parking lot and, even then, she continued.

I shifted up into fourth and I felt her breath leave her chest in a rush.

I smiled when I saw the red light ahead, shifting down into third when I wouldn't usually downshift.

Her pussy was so hot that I felt the heat radiating off her through her jeans onto my hand.

By the time we arrived at the parking lot, I'd not even heard the last five minutes of conversation.

Which was why the minute I exited the car, she surprised me with the topic of conversation.

"When I was fifteen, my best friend and I thought it'd be a good idea to break into our school to save the cats we were dissecting the next day," Raven started, hefting up two bags in her good hand and starting for the stairs.

I picked up the rest of them and started after her, passing her on the stairs to make it to her apartment first.

Placing the sacks on the floor, I held my hands out for the keys.

"Why would you do that?" I asked. "They're already dead."

She handed me the keys and followed closely behind me as I walked into her place.

I checked all of the rooms and walked to the kitchen where I put her keys down on the counter in front of her.

She finally replied, picking the keys up and tossing them in the general vicinity of her purse, which was still on the couch.

"We knew they were already dead," she amended. "What we didn't know was that the school had an alarm."

I blinked, leaning my hip against the counter.

"Every smart person would put an alarm in their house to protect themselves," I informed her.

She stuck her tongue out once again, and my cock jumped in my pants.

I looked down at said cock, and realized that she would be able to see it if she dropped her eyes in that direction.

Luckily, she was too busy putting away her groceries to notice my hard on.

"We got in, lugged as many frozen cats out that we could, and were all the way at the back of the property when the first cop car came."

"They arrest you?" I cut in.

She shook her head.

"No. Jessie and I ran," she smiled whimsically. "Never caught us."

"What was the point of this story?" I wondered aloud.

She narrowed her eyes at me and tossed an empty plastic bag at my face.

"You forgot to bring my beer in," she said haughtily.

I grinned and started for the door.

"Make sure you offer Mig an invitation to eat when you go down there," Raven yelled at my retreating back.

I stopped and turned to look at her.

"You saw him?" I asked.

She nodded, grinning.

Shaking my head, I made my way out of her apartment, my eyes scanning the darkness surrounding the parking lot as I went.

The moment my feet hit level ground, Mig's silent form appeared beside me.

"Anything?" I asked.

"Not a damn thing," he replied. "I'm headed home."

"Annie call?" I asked.

He shook his head.

"No. My mom's keeping her busy," he replied. "Gotta get home to check on the dogs."

I laughed.

Mig had gotten a new dog about a month ago. A new dog who was pregnant, unbeknownst to Mig, when he picked her out. A very pregnant new dog, who had puppies about a week or so after he brought her home.

When Mig had tried to take them back, Annie had thrown the mother of all hissy fits saying that she'd 'bonded' with the dogs, making it nearly impossible to get rid of them.

"You got the tests run on them, didn't you?" I asked.

He nodded.

"One hundred percent Golden Retrievers. When I called the previous owners about the dog that knocked her up, they asked to have her back since they didn't realize that the pregnancy took. I told them no, and they refused to hand over the info on the male," he explained.

I snorted.

"Fucking lucky," I said. "And I'm assuming you found the sire?"

Mig gave me a Cheshire cat grin.

"I sure as fuck did," he said. "Gave the owner of the sire pick of the litter like he was promised, and I got the papers from him to sell the puppies. Five hundred bucks a pup is the *lowest* they sell for. These dogs, though, were of championship lines, meaning I can sell the puppies for upwards of a grand if I could only get Annie to let go of them."

"She's not going to let you," I promised him.

He snorted. "Don't I know it. Anyway, gotta go."

I waved him off and grabbed the beer out of the back of the truck before taking the steps two at a time.

The moment I opened the door to Raven's apartment, my stomach immediately jumped in anticipation at the smell that greeted me.

Lani Lynn Vale

CHAPTER 6

The beer and the beard made me do it.
-Raven's secret thoughts

Wolf

"What are you making?" I asked her as I moved around the counter that separated her living room from the kitchen.

"Give me one of those," she ordered, holding out her casted hand. "And Alice Spring's Chicken. I actually do make this one dish. But, that's really the extent of my culinary talents."

"Smells fuckin' awesome. Mig can't eat." I ripped open the box and handed her one before taking the case to the fridge.

She stopped me before I could make it all the way.

"You're staying, right?" she asked.

Was that hopefulness I heard in her voice?

I nodded my head. "Sure am."

"I got your favorite beer." She pointed.

My brows rose.

"How'd you know that cheap beer was my favorite?" I challenged.

I knew how she knew. It was the same reason I knew she liked tacos better than fajitas. I also knew her favorite soft drink was Mountain Dew.

Her favorite alcoholic drink was a glass of wine that was so sweet that it didn't even taste like it was alcoholic.

She gave me a look.

"Your sister told me," she said distractedly. "Although it's not hard to figure out after watching you drink it every time you came over to your sister's house, or when you went out to dinner with us."

"Why'd you leave?" I asked her, placing the case into the fridge and grabbing a can before turning back to her to gauge her reaction to my question.

She grimaced and looked away.

"Why?" I asked again when she still didn't explain.

"Everything good or healthy has a way of turning unhealthy around me," she replied. "It was better to leave before it turned bad."

I cracked the top on the can of beer and took a healthy swallow before placing it on the counter and walking to her.

She had her back to me, doing some weird shit with the chicken breasts in between a plastic bag with a rolling pin.

Placing one hand on each side of her hips, I waited until she finally sighed.

"It's better this way, I swear," she promised.

I waited until she growled in frustration.

"You, okay?" I said.

"It was because of you."

My heart squeezed. "Why me?" I asked, lifting my hand to sweep some of the stray hairs that'd fallen from her ponytail off her neck.

I dropped my lips so they rested on the muscle of her shoulder, and she shivered.

Lips skimming her shoulder blade, I smiled when she finally replied.

"You make me do this." She lifted her shoulders in a shrug.

"You're not making sense," I whispered against her skin.

She shivered.

"You. I left because of you. You have a son. You have a woman. You have a family. I didn't like being there." She cleared her throat and dropped the knife she was using to cut up the chicken. "You make me wish for things that'll never be. It hurts to be around you."

I inhaled deeply, then stepped back until our bodies were no longer touching.

I pulled the beer up to my lips, then drained it.

"You shouldn't have left," I whispered to her gratingly.

"Why?" she asked, perplexed.

"Because I didn't want you to. I've been thinking about you since you were rescued."

I hadn't intended for those thoughts to ever leave the confines of my lips.

In fact, the last fucking thing in the world Raven needed right then was my fucked-up self in her life.

I'd always been trailer trash. A useless sack of bones—or so every single one of my high school teachers had informed me throughout my high school career.

The only thing that'd saved my life was enlisting in the Marines at the age of eighteen.

I'd met my wife the moment I got out of the Marines, ten years later, and had fallen in love with her—or the idea of her.

I should've never pursued her. Look where that got her. Six feet under, decomposing and feeding the worms due to my career choice.

I'd always been a selfish bastard, though.

Which was why I was about to do something the both of us might regret come morning.

My hand holding the beer can let it go, and it fell to the ground at our feet, clacking against the tiled floor like a shot resounding off the empty walls of a firing range.

Raven would've jumped and turned…if I'd let her.

Which I didn't.

I held her still, immobile against the counter with not just my hands at her hips, but my pelvis against her backside.

"Wolf," she whispered, panic starting to rise in her voice.

I placed my lips against the top of her head and inhaled deeply, taking in the hint of cucumbers and something else that I couldn't quite place.

"Raven," I whispered.

Backing up until a good four feet separated us, I waited for her to turn.

The moment she did, my breath caught in my throat.

My eyes ran up and down her body, taking everything in with one glance.

"Those shorts you were wearing earlier were fucking sexy as hell, but those jeans you somehow painted on are making it hard to breathe," I told her, my eyes taking everything in at once.

She smiled timidly.

"These aren't usually what I wear out," she whispered. "Wolf…what are you doing? What are we doing here?"

I grinned at her.

"What do you want to do?" I asked.

She smiled softly, her face blushing a deep red before she shook her head and refused to answer.

"You don't want to know what I want to do," she challenged me, her eyes locking with mine. "You'd probably not appreciate it."

"Try me," I challenged her.

She licked her lips.

"I remember."

My eyes slammed shut, and I shuttered at the remembrance of just what exactly she could 'remember.'

"What do you 'remember'?" I whispered gruffly.

Her eyes lifted from the contemplation of my chest, and she gasped for air.

"What you did for me. The night you found me. What you did. I remember. Everything," she choked out.

My eyes closed, remembering the horror of seeing Raven that way, but also remembering how she felt in my arms as I carried her out of that nightmare.

Her eyes filled with tears as she relived the memories of that time.

"He tortured me. It wasn't the same way as he tortured July, but he did it all the same," she confirmed my worst fears.

"I sure as hell won't ever forget that night," I said gruffly.

She shook her head, refusing to give me any more information than what she already had.

I moved forward until there was only a breath separating her from me.

She leaned forward and rested her head against my chest, my heart thumping with the emotion of that night and this one.

CHAPTER 7

*Why are there so many warning labels on things? What happened
to survival of the fittest?*
-Wolf's secret thoughts

Raven

1 year ago

I peeled open my eyes.

In a different place, again.

Wonderful.

*"Let me out, your stupid asshole!" I screamed, my voice raw and
unsteady.*

That was usual for me.

It wasn't very often that I knew where I was anymore.

Jensen liked to drug me and move me where he wanted me.

*He also liked to incapacitate me and do things to my body when he
couldn't get it from anyone else.*

I, of course, deserved it.

*I'd given him access to my body before, so why wouldn't he be able to
keep accessing it, right?*

Then I viciously shut that thought down.

Jesus Christ! This was not okay. Him touching me while I was drugged out of my mind was not okay!

I didn't want this!

I was on my knees, naked, my hands tied above my head, holding my body up even though everything inside of me wanted to collapse in exhaustion on the floor. And he had a vibrator strapped to me.

My stomach churned at what was happening to me.

"Fuck!" I heard Jensen cry from the side of the room. "We gotta go. We're fucking surrounded by cops."

"Those aren't cops," Barrett, the other captor in this whole fucked up mess, explained. "Are you done with your play toy? Can we go?"

"Yeah, we can go," Jensen said. Then he dropped down to his haunches across from me, his eyes level with mine. "You saw what happened to July."

It wasn't a question, but a statement. A threat.

I nodded in confirmation.

It was likely something I'd never forget.

I'd seen the whole thing, and it tore at my heart, even all this time later.

But, time was relative when you were kidnapped.

When you had nothing else to do but sit there and think, the passage of time became so inconsequential that it was nearly humorous.

Nearly.

Jensen got up and started across the room and tears started to leak out of my eyes.

The tears weren't for Jensen.

They were for me.

For the fact that, yet again, he was going to leave me hanging.

Only this time he was leaving me hanging with an end in sight. That end being the possibility of discovery, of rescue. The possibility of others seeing me in this position, seeing what Jensen was doing to me, seeing my shame.

A possibility that became a reality not five minutes later when the darkest, most beautiful man I had ever seen entered.

His eyes zeroed in on me.

In an instant, he had me catalogued.

Hands above my head. Naked as the day I was born. Vibrator shoved up my vagina being held in place with a black belt.

My eyes closed in mortification as the man came straight to me while ordering everyone else out of the room.

"Are you okay?" he asked.

I nodded my head, my heart practically galloping in my chest.

Could he hear the vibrator?

I knew he could.

It was near impossible for him not to hear it.

He dropped to his knees so his eyes were level with mine.

"Can I remove it?" the man with the black eyes and the intimidating set of shoulders asked me.

My eyes lifted to his, and the blush of my humiliation burned on my cheeks.

I nodded my head.

"Please," I croaked, my voice cracking.

He next went to work removing the belt and pulling out the vibrator. Then went on to the bindings on my hands and quickly untied me. He pulled off the shirt he was wearing and wrapped it around my naked body, lifting me into his arms and swiftly carrying me out of hell.

And then he held me while I cried.

The *tap tap tap* of someone knocking had me jolting in bed, and I looked around in confusion at my surroundings.

That's when I realized that I wasn't by myself in my bed. I was on top of someone.

A very muscular someone.

"You're going to be late if you don't get up now!" Travis called through my door.

"I'll be late. I'll drive myself," I yelled at Travis, hoping he didn't use his key like he normally did when he thought I was sleeping in.

I had a problem waking up in the morning.

He knew it. I knew it.

However, he must've interpreted the wakefulness in my voice because he didn't try to come inside like he would've done had I not sounded awake.

"Oh, God," I breathed, pushing back until I could see the chest that'd been my human pillow for who knew how long.

Wolf's eyes were awake and aware, focused solidly on me.

"What are you doing?" I asked frantically, my eyes going down the length of our bodies.

Luckily, we both were still fully clothed, meaning we'd not done anything he could regret later.

That thought flew out the window moments later when he suddenly reversed our positions and I was underneath of him.

"What are you doing?" I asked him, watching him with wide eyes.

"Leaving," he murmured.

A smile broke out on my face.

"It sure does look like you're leaving," I murmured sarcastically, eyeing his face from only a few inches away from my own.

"Gotta work myself up to it."

"Why?" I asked.

"Because it's eight forty-two and I can hear men talking downstairs, which likely means Travis and Dante are here already. Therefore, I'll have to walk through all of them to get to my truck, a truck they helped me restore so there is no doubt they know exactly who owns it," he informed me.

My mouth dropped open.

"Are you embarrassed to be seen with me?" I asked him in outrage.

He shook his head.

"No," he murmured. "What I'm embarrassed about is conking out after only two beers."

"So that means…what?" I asked. "That you would've gotten out of here earlier, but you were too drunk to do so?"

He grinned.

"You're taking everything I say out of context."

I bared my teeth at him, causing a grin to spread over his face.

"I'm going to go to work. What I don't want to do is go out there and see Dante and Travis look at me like they looked at me yesterday morning when they realized I knew you better than they knew you."

My held breath left me in a whoosh when I realized that he wasn't actually embarrassed to be seen with me.

"Gotta go, babe. Make sure you stay with Travis or Dante. Don't leave to get them lunch. Don't run to the grocery store for a cookie. Don't ..." I held my hand up to stop him.

"We went over this last night," I reminded him.

Wolf grinned and pushed off of the bed, and I lost his warmth.

The feeling it left me with wasn't one I particularly liked, and to cover it up, I got up as well and quickly changed out of the shirt I'd worn all day yesterday.

The pants would stay. Those weren't anything but nice and stretched out now, so there was no reason to change them. It was rare that these pants ever felt anything but tight.

I heard the bathroom sink switch on and I yanked the first t-shirt down from the hanger, not even noticing which one it was until it was too late to change.

The bathroom door opened just as the shirt passed over my ribs, and I didn't pretend for a second to miss the sharp inhalation of breath that passed over Wolf's lips at seeing my bare back.

"When did you get that tattoo?" he asked hoarsely.

His voice sounded rough, and I couldn't quite tell why he sounded like that.

"The week before I left Kilgore," I whispered, turning to face him.

The moment I turned, though, he turned me back around and lifted my shirt.

"Exact fucking replication in reverse," he murmured, running his rough hands over the tattoo that stretched the length of one half of my back.

"What is?" I questioned him, turning even though his hand was still busy running along my back.

Without answering me, he turned and gave me his back, and I gasped.

"That's so cool!" I whispered.

He grinned at me over his shoulder.

"You don't see the significance here?" he asked me, dropping his shirt back into place and leaving me feeling bereft at not getting to see that beautiful back of his anymore.

Then what he said struck home, and my mouth opened and closed like a guppy.

"You have a raven on your back! And I have a wolf!" I crowed. "Why do you have a raven?" I looked at him in confusion.

"The week before you left, I got this. Because of your strength," he said. "You reminded me of things I couldn't change. Things I needed to move on from."

He must've seen my face at the mention of him moving on from me, because he was quick to explain.

"Not moving on from you, but everything in general. My wife mostly, but even more my way of life. I wasn't living. In fact, I was so far from living that it was almost comical. It took seeing you, so vulnerable and broken that tipped those scales for me, and made me realize that I needed to get my life together. That's what this symbolizes." He patted his shoulder where the tattoo rested.

It was big, not just a small tattoo of a raven on his body.

No, this one looked so real, so lifelike and big, that if you were standing far away, it could literally pass as a real-life raven.

The beak and neck of the raven stretched from Wolf's muscled shoulder all the way down to right above his collarbone. One side of the wings of the raven went down underneath the raven's head, cutting across his chest and coming to a stop right between his nipples, while the other wing flared down the length of his back. The raven's tail and feet ran down the length of his arm and stopped right around where his bicep started.

It was very intricate and well done, and oh so beautiful.

Hauntingly so.

"Let me see yours again," Wolf said. "All of it."

I presented him my back and lifted my shirt up to rest at the top of my neck, pulling one arm out of the sleeve to give him full access.

The next thing to go was the bra, which Wolf oh so helpfully unlatched for me.

I barely caught the cups from dislodging my breasts in time.

The mirror on my closet door showed his mirth at the near slip, and I narrowed my eyes at him.

"Rude."

He grinned and I lost his eyes as they took in every last inch of my tattoo.

I knew what he was looking at.

I was surprised myself at how beautiful it was.

And big.

It was most definitely big. *Realllly big.*

The thing about the tattoo that I loved the most, though, were the eyes.

They were Wolf's eyes.

I wasn't sure if he noticed that, but it was the one thing that I adored most about the entire piece.

I hadn't got it because of Wolf specifically. It was more as a dedication to him, though. A dedication to myself and a release from the shitty life

I'd lived.

Wolf was my starting over point. From the moment he set me free, I started a new life. One where I intended to live it, not caring what or who I pissed off to make sure I lived it the way I wanted to live it.

I was a lone wolf. I only had me to count on.

Or, at the time I got the tattoo, that'd been my reasoning behind getting it.

My 'official' reason, anyway.

I'd be lying to myself if I said Wolf didn't play a bigger part in the decision to get this particular tattoo, though.

"It has my eyes."

My lids dropped and I breathed out before inhaling deeply.

"It was a reminder."

I heard him chuckle behind his back, and just when he was about to say something, his phone rang, interrupting his thoughts.

"Hello?" Wolf answered gruffly. "You're kidding me, right? At the fucking Dairy Queen on Fourth?"

I strapped my bra closed and pulled my t-shirt back to rights before turning around and surveying the man behind me.

His hair was mussed from sleep, and his beard was poofier than usual, making me reach forward almost on autopilot to smooth it down.

He grinned at the feel of my hand on his beard, and I couldn't help the shiver of anticipation that poured through me at feeling something so intimate on Wolf's body.

If I could make his beard into my lucky rabbit's foot and hang it from my keychain, you wouldn't find my hand empty with all the good luck rubbing I'd be doing.

Alas, that wasn't possible, and he pulled away from me only to pull me snugly into his body.

"I have to go," he informed me like I hadn't just heard his phone call that I'd garnered just as much from. "A man I've been looking for is eating breakfast at the Dairy Queen two towns over. Be safe, and don't leave without…"

I held up my hand.

"You don't have to repeat yourself that many times. I heard you the first time," I crossed my arms over my chest.

Wolf's eyes followed my movement, and his gaze lingered on my chest for a long moment before he nodded once, then proceeded to walk out of the door.

I could do nothing but shake my head at his abrupt departure.

With nothing else left to do, and an itching need to get the hell out of my apartment that still smelled like Wolf, I grabbed my boots, shoved my feet into them without socks, and called Marky Mark to me.

"You'll have to go to work with me today, buddy. I'm sure that's okay with you, right?" I asked my best buddy.

Marky Mark looked up at me with dark gray eyes, and I smiled.

"Yeah, I thought so."

CHAPTER 8

Every man has a bad boy in him. It all depends on whether or not there's been a reason for the bad boy to be awakened in him.
-Fact of life

Wolf

"Get. The. Fuck. Off. Me," I growled, pushing at the two fuckers that were trying to beat me senseless. "Get off me!"

With a final burst of strength, I rolled my hips to the left, and then swung my entire body to the left, dislodging the one on my feet, as well as the one on my upper body.

They both lost their grip.

They didn't get far before they were trying to subdue me once again, but the momentary reprieve I'd been given was enough, and I fought like a rabid animal to get loose completely.

The moment my feet hit solid ground again, I pulled my gun out of my holster underneath my armpit, aimed at the first guy, and shot him in the chest.

The right side of his chest, not the left.

I was considerate, and don't let anyone ever tell you different.

"Don't fucking move!" I yelled at the other guy who'd rolled over and started to reach for his holster at his side.

The man froze and moved his hands up in the air, his eyes wide and alarmed.

"Yeah, you stupid fucker," I growled in anger. "You should be scared."

Reaching carefully down for my discarded phone on the concrete next to the bleeding man, I pulled it up, unlocked it with my thumbprint, and immediately dialed Ridley.

Except the moment Ridley answered, he growled, "Your fucking woman you asked me to keep an eye on is fucking crazy as shit!"

"I'm not crazy and I'm not stressed! And I'm not being overly dramatic!" Raven yelled. "Fuck you! I was just shot at! Again!"

My heart started to lurch at hearing the fear in Raven's voice.

"Let me talk to him! God! Leave me alone!" Raven bellowed.

The sound of the phone being transferred from Ridley to someone else had my brows raising.

The girl had a way about her, that was for sure.

"Sir, we're going to have to ask you to come down here and take her somewhere," the new holder of the phone, and one of Ridley's fellow officers, said.

I heard a deep male voice that sounded like Ridley's over the line, and then Raven yelling again.

"No! You want to know what's dramatic?" I guessed she was waiting for some sort of reply, because the moment I heard Ridley's rumble of 'no, what?' Raven said, "When an octopus gets overly-stressed, it eats itself. Now that is dramatic. I think me screaming and crying isn't anywhere near as bad as it could get."

I grinned, which seemed to set the man off that I was holding the gun on.

He moved, throwing his body toward mine, and in an instant, I'd discharged my service weapon for the second time in less than a minute.

"Sir," the officer yelled.

All yelling from the opposite end of the line halted, and I stared with detached fascination as the man's lifeless body crumpled to the floor at my feet, nearly on top of the other fallen man's body.

"I'll need a Justice of the Peace as well as a few cars at my location," I informed him. "I'm two blocks south of..."

***

"What the fuck, man?" Ridley asked. "You told me I only had to watch her. You didn't say a goddamn thing about her getting shot at. They shot my new cruiser! Do you know how long it took the county to fucking get me this one back?"

I looked at him like he'd lost his mind.

"I'm not being a bitch!" Ridley yelled, waving his arms for emphasis.

"Could've fooled me," Raven muttered darkly.

Ridley's eyes narrowed, and he took a threatening step towards her.

"What did I tell you about talking?" Ridley snapped.

"That I have an annoying voice, and you want me to shut up so you can think?" Raven offered.

My mouth dropped open.

"What? Are you PMSing or something?" I asked him. "What's your malfunction?"

"My malfunction is that I missed an important meeting with the fucking mayor of three cities because I was busy being shot at!"

I blinked.

"That's it?" I asked.

Ridley sneered at me.

"This is about your wife, isn't it?" I tried.

Ridley's body became wired.

"What'd you do to her?" I teased him. "Forget to mow the lawn? Got home late?"

Ridley sighed.

"Forgot to pick up my dry cleaning, and now I have to wear these shitty pants that are too small," he grumbled.

I would not laugh. I would not laugh.

"Are those stretchy?" Raven asked, leaning down to inspect Ridley's pants.

Ridley stepped back, but the damage was already done.

"Take her somewhere. Bring her back tomorrow to get her statement taken," he ordered.

Grimacing to myself, I nodded my confirmation, then watched as Ridley left.

My eyes were drawn to his pants, though, and I couldn't help but wonder if they were indeed stretchy.

The two men's blood decorating the concrete was being washed away as I walked Raven to my truck.

My breath, however, stalled in my chest the moment we got to the passenger side door.

My mood, already not in the best of places, deteriorated when I got my first good look at my truck and saw the bullet holes in the door.

"Mother Fucker," I growled.

Then I turned to say something to Raven, and got my first good look at what she was wearing, and every single man in a five-mile radius checking out her assets.

***

Raven

"That's inconvenient," I replied at seeing the previously pristine paint.

Now it had two large holes in the door panel with chipped paint peeling an inch past the holes.

"It looks like an actual bullet hole does on the TV," I said, not able to stop my mouth.

It was a character flaw. I babbled incessantly when I was nervous.

I also babbled when I wasn't, just a bit less though.

This time was one of those times when I really should've shut up.

"God, I'm hungry," I said as I climbed into his truck. "Where are you taking me?"

Wolf followed me inside and started the truck.

Without a second thought, I parted my legs and kept chatting as Wolf started the truck up.

He backed out of the parking spot as I prattled on about how surprising it was that we'd both had shots fired at us at the same time.

"It wasn't a coincidence," Wolf muttered as he dropped the truck into second and pulled out of the parking lot. "Where do you want to eat?"

I pursed my lips.

"Fast food will be fine. Just nothing that has to do with Italian. I don't think I could handle the red sauce at this point in time," I said honestly.

Honesty was obviously not the way to go, because he growled under his breath.

"Would you please stop talking," he muttered darkly.

I zipped my lips and started to count to one hundred in my head.

I'd gotten to fifteen when he dropped the shifter into my crotch...I mean fourth.

I jumped and parted my legs wider in hopes that the ball of the shifter didn't touch my clit like that, but the skirt I was wearing wasn't conducive with spreading my legs as wide as I would need to get his hand out of my pussy.

So I sat there, with his hand on the shifter on my crotch, until we arrived in the parking lot of the diner that was on the outskirts of Uncertain.

I'd always liked Uncertain.

It was an absolutely beautiful place, even though the area had been ravaged from the storms and flooding a few weeks prior, it looked just as beautiful as ever, despite the water still being up as high as it was.

Wolf got out and held his hand out for me, grabbing mine so I could climb out without flashing him completely.

I didn't need to bother hiding anything, though, because his eyes were on the parking lot and not me.

I'd just stood up and started to push my skirt down my legs when he tugged my hand, slammed the door to the truck, and started walking all in five seconds flat.

"Slow down, you long-legged monster," I growled, tugging on my hand.

He slowed his pace, but didn't say a word of apology as we made our way to the door.

He pulled the door open for me and I preceded him inside, my eyes on the diner around me.

It was one of those old timey feeling diners that was just one long room. Although this one was unique in a sense due to the train that was running around the top of the ceiling around the entire room.

The bottom half of the walls were black and white subway tiles while the floor sported the same checkered patterns, only in linoleum.

The top half of the walls were painted a bright red that was nearly headache inducing, and the tables and chairs all matched the black, white, and red theme they had going on.

"Two?" an older lady asked.

"Yes," Wolf clipped.

I rolled my eyes and followed behind Wolf, wondering just what in the hell I was doing.

The moment we sat down I knew I should've asked him to take me home and not to a public restaurant where every single person in the entire establishment was watching us and every move we made.

"What's everyone's deal?" I asked Wolf.

He looked up, and his eyes were full of anger.

"Fucking people like seeing spectacles, and that's exactly what you are right now," he growled.

My mouth dropped open.

"What?" I asked, surprise and astonishment clear in my voice.

"That fucking skirt you're wearing is so short I can see the yellow happy face underwear you're wearing," he grumbled.

I looked down to check, and sure enough I could see the yellow underwear.

"Okay," I said. "But that was because you watched me get out of the car. Not because I'm giving you some kind of peep show."

His mouth tightened, and his eyes slithered to the side as the waiter showed asking for our drink orders.

Forty-five minutes later, I was ready to kill him.

"You don't need the burger. Let's go," Wolf growled in annoyance.

I froze in the process of taking the to-go container from the server.

"I don't *need* the burger?" I asked carefully.

Wolf, oblivious to the dangerous territory he'd just entered into, continued to run his stupid mouth.

"No," he said. "There's no point for you to take a little itty bitty hamburger home. That's not even a proper meal. That's more like a snack or something to that effect. It's just enough to remind you that you want more, and you can't have it."

I carefully opened the Styrofoam box as the server, a young woman around my age, looked at me sympathetically, shook her head, and left.

Placing my burger into the large partition in the box, which I admit was on the small side since I'd eaten most of it, I glared at Wolf.

"Ready," I said carefully, trying not to betray my anger.

Wolf stood up with barely contained impatience.

"If you didn't want to go to dinner with me, you should've just said," I growled at Wolf's retreating back.

Wolf didn't slow until he came to the front entrance. Holding the door open to the little diner he'd stopped to take me to, he glared at me.

"I wanted to eat just as much as you did," he muttered.

I chose to be silent the rest of the way. There was no way in hell I was going to bug him when he was acting like he was.

I didn't know what the deal with him was, and to be honest, I didn't really care.

I'd had a bad damn day. Again.

I'd been fired. I was now practically homeless.

Thankfully, though, Travis had offered to help me move into his rental house across town from where I was staying, but I didn't want any fucking handouts.

If I wasn't working there anymore, then there was no fucking point in getting the discounted rate that Travis was trying to still offer me.

Which now meant I was job searching and house hunting.

During my house hunting/job search, I'd had a call from the sheriff, a man I'd never met before, asking me where the hell I was.

Apparently, I was supposed to be somewhere with him, and I hadn't showed.

Thinking something was wrong and I hadn't been informed, I'd rushed to the sheriff's office only to be shot at in the parking lot on my walk inside.

The moment the shots rang out I'd been taken down from behind by that bear, the sheriff, now known to me as Ridley.

Needless to say, I was not in a good mood.

I'd had a very shitty, no good, God awful, very bad day.

And now he was handing me shit that I didn't need to deal with.

"I want to go home," I murmured angrily.

Wolf gave me a look that clearly said what he thought about me going home.

"Like I'd take you back to your place after how well Travis looked out for you today. No. You're going to my place."

I decided not to argue with him.

Maybe after he cooled off, I could reason with him.

But halfway during his drive home he got a call that clearly took precedence over what he was doing.

"Fuck me," he growled, swinging his truck around to head in the opposite direction.

I told myself not to ask, but my curiosity got the better of me.

"What's going on?" I asked.

"One of the men I've been using as an informant was shot tonight and is at the county hospital," he murmured darkly.

When we arrived at my apartment and got out of the car, I hurried up the steps, but even as fast as my legs were moving Wolf still beat me.

He opened the door with the key out of my hand, and made a quick but thorough sweep through the house.

While he was doing that. I put my hamburger in the fridge and watched him move.

Once he was appeased, he stopped in front of me, and then yanked me to him.

"I'm going to tell Travis to pull his head out of his ass and watch over you. Don't leave the apartment. I'll be back."

Without giving me a chance to argue, he was gone, leaving me shivering as his body heat dissipated from my side.

"Goddammit," I breathed. "What are you doing to me, Wolf?"

Of course nobody answered, and I had no answers for that burning question.

Lani Lynn Vale

CHAPTER 9

I'm not the girl that everyone loves, but at least I'm not the girl that everyone has had.
-Raven's secret thoughts

Raven

I woke to the smell of him on my sheets, and the imprint of his head on my pillow.

At some point during the night he must have returned, and now, at seven fifty in the morning, he was gone again.

And so was my fucking hamburger. Although I didn't realize that until much later as I was dreaming about it.

My day started like any other.

I got up. Washed my face. Brushed my hair and then threw it up into a sloppy bun on the top of my head.

Then, for the hell of it, I put a load of laundry into the washer and pulled the cold ones from the dryer.

After folding them and putting them in my suitcase, I started to gather my belongings.

The bedroom was where I started, and since the entirety of the apartment was furnished when I moved in, the only thing I had to grab from in here were my sheets, my clothes, and my shoes.

The bathroom was just as easy. Since nothing beside the shower curtain (which you bet your ass I grabbed) and the hair care products, makeup, and toilet cleaners were mine, it was easy to shove them into another bag I'd previously used for the gym.

Then I moved to the living room that really didn't have much other than a few magazines.

Magazines that could stay.

While I was contemplating what to do with said magazines, toss them or hang every single page up on the wall that had anything suggestive to it at all, I heard a knock at my door.

I glared at it, knowing in my heart it was Travis, and growled.

Checking the peephole to confirm my suspicion, I yanked it open and glared at the man who looked like he hadn't ripped my life apart the day before.

"I'm sorry," he said the moment he saw my face.

I shrugged.

"I'm getting out of here by tonight," I said. "What do you want?"

Travis brows furrowed.

"Have you given anymore thought to the rental house? The occupants just left yesterday; likely it'll need to be cleaned first," he explained.

I shook my head.

"I'm not staying at your rental house if I'm not working for you," I refused stubbornly.

I wasn't a person that accepted handouts. Handouts came with expectations that I'll owe the person that gave me the handout someday.

I wasn't that kind of person. If I wasn't earning it beforehand, I wouldn't take the handout, simple as that.

And if I wasn't working for Travis and Dante, I wasn't living in their house.

No excuses.

"Why not?" he asked.

I glared at the man.

He was sexy, that was for sure.

His head of brown hair and ice blue eyes didn't hold a candle to Wolf, though, and that rankled.

"Because I don't want to be beholden to you for a handout that I can't begin to pay back," I replied.

"So where will you go?" he asked, confusion that I wasn't taking what he had to offer.

"I'm going back home, I guess," I responded, despondency leaching into my voice even though I didn't want it to.

My money that I'd saved during the trial was gone.

I'd gotten complacent here.

Bought new clothes.

Paid off my debts and put a down payment on my piece of shit car.

And it was a piece of shit. My piece of shit, but still a piece of shit, nonetheless.

"You can't go home," he replied. "You don't have a home to go home to."

I did have a home to go home to. In fact, I had two. Although both places were in separate towns.

The first one was the same place I'd been staying in while I was in Kilgore awaiting Jensen's trial. It was the same place that July owned that was across the street from the place where July and PD had made their home.

I'd been the only one to live in it, and I got the invitation from July on a weekly basis to come back and stay in it. For some reason, she was holding it vacant for me in case I wanted to come back, and even now, after four months of me being gone, she still had it at the ready and waiting for me.

The other place I could go was back home to Karnack.

I had a home there.

I paid for it. It wasn't much, just a two-bedroom shotgun house that was the size of a Cracker Jack box.

There was a couple renting it from me on a monthly basis, and they were on a month-to-month lease, I just had to give them ten days' notice to vacate if I needed it back.

They were fine with those terms, and it worked for me.

I gave them the rent for a song on the condition that they would move out of the house if I ever needed it. They also did the upkeep and any repairs that were needed on the house if any were to ever arise.

See, I had options!

"I have places I can go," I replied without giving him any information to go on.

His eyes narrowed.

"You can't stay with Wolf. He'll ruin your life," Travis said so viciously that I took a step back.

"What are you talking about?" I asked.

His eyes narrowed.

"That's who you're going to stay with, isn't it?" he asked. "I'm serious. Wolf likes to ruin lives, one broken heart at a time."

I smiled a tad bit evilly at him.

"You're not my brother, Travis. You're my employer, or ex-employer. I can stay with whomever I want, and if that includes a man that went out of his way to make sure that I survived, then I'll sure as hell do it. Because I'm an adult, and I can make my own informed decisions if I have to," I growled.

Travis' eyebrows lifted. "Don't come crawling back here when he ruins you."

I laughed.

"Fuck off," I said. "And go away so I can finish packing."

Travis sighed.

"This wasn't what I intended for today. I was going to offer you the option of working from home, but Wolf makes me pissed off on the best of days and I can't think clearly when it comes to him." Travis crossed his arms and looked toward the living room window, his eyes scanning the yard. "When I saw him leave your place yesterday morning, I was just so pissed off that he took another good woman and ruined her life."

"I ruined my own life by hooking up with a guy that was a piece of shit," I told him honestly. "I wish that was different, but it's not. It was my own stupidity that got me into that position, and I can't change the fact. Wolf, however, did nothing wrong. He's given me every opportunity to get my life back, and I owe him more than you'll ever know."

Travis' face contorted.

"He killed my sister."

I smiled at him sympathetically.

"I read the newspaper article," I said. "I also got it firsthand from his sister, as well as quite a few other individuals. He didn't kill anyone. If anything, it was he who suffered the most with this. You lost your sister. He, however, lost his wife, his unborn child, his best friend, and his best friend's wife." I looked at him as I opened the door and gestured for him to leave.

He skittered past me without looking back, but when his foot was on the last step that led down to the forecourt of Hail Auto Recovery I called to him.

"Travis."

He looked at me over his shoulder.

"He misses you."

Travis' head dropped.

"He hasn't said as much, but it took a lot of courage for him to come here and ask you for your help. The least you could do is give him that help when it obviously doesn't cost you a damn thing to do it." I licked my lips. "You're a good man, Travis. Don't get sucked in by Dante's bad attitude and stoop down to his level."

And it was Dante.

Something more had happened between Dante and Wolf.

Something that Wolf had yet to expound on, and Dante refused to share.

I'd figure it out, though, and when I did, I'd fix them all.

It was obvious that there was lost love between them.

That much hate didn't come about without there having been a little bit of love there first.

When I could no longer see Travis, I closed the door and went to the kitchen, freezing the moment my eyes lit on the counter.

The first sign that something was wrong with my hamburger was the to-go box on the counter, and the crumbs on the counter where he must've stood while he ate it.

"Oh no he didn't."

Raven (10:03 AM): Open your door. I have a bone to pick with you.

Raven (10:04 AM): Where are you? I seriously am about to have a fucking conniption fit. I cannot believe you did this to me!

Raven (10:05 AM): You either open your door or I'm going to steal your wreath.

Wolf (1:03 PM): Oh, no! Not my wreath!

Raven (1:03 PM): Your wreath is gone. I put it on someone's grave on the way home.

Wolf (2:14 PM): My sister put that wreath there.

Raven (2:14 PM): I also took something else. I hope you trip and fall on your face.

Wolf (4:14 PM): Shaking in my boots.

Raven (4:14 PM): You will be. Bitch.

Wolf (7:14 PM): I don't know what you did with it, but you will bring it back. It better be in the same condition I left it in, or you will pay. I will find you. Then I will kill you.

Raven (3:14 AM): Fuck you.

Raven (4:14 AM): You suck.

Raven (4:17 AM): I can't sleep. What are you doing?

Raven (4:22 AM): Seriously, are you sleeping?

Raven (4:33 AM): I left your bike by the supermarket with a for sale sign on it. I hope it's still there when I go look for it in the morning.

Wolf (4:33 AM): It damn well better be or I'll take it out on your ass.

Raven (4:34 AM): So you are awake.

Grinning, I shut my phone off, and then walked to the bed where I fell face first into it.

Groaning as the bed seemed to swallow me whole, I closed my eyes and buried my head into the thousand thread count sheets, the very thing that the hotel I'd decided to stay at boasted of.

After spending the last seven hours job searching since a certain someone let me go from my job claiming that it was no longer safe for his other employees for me to be there, I went a little mad.

Then I'd splurged on an expensive hotel room, paying in cash, thinking it would keep the vultures at bay.

Clearly, I hadn't been giving Wolf the credit he deserved.

I didn't find that out until much later in the night, though.

Once I'd laid there for over an hour contemplating my life, I got up and showered– which, might I add, was still hard after dozens of showers. Putting a trash bag over my arm was for the birds. I hope I never break my arm again, because it blows.

Then I'd rented a movie on Pay-Per-View, a dirty one, and promptly fell asleep before I got to the good part.

It was the breeze on my bare back that woke me.

It wasn't much, just a small whisper of air, but it was enough to make me crack my eyes open and see what was going on around me.

The screen across the room from me was just getting to the good part, which meant I hadn't been asleep for long.

The man had the woman on her back, his hips between hers, and he was rubbing the length of his dick against the lips of her sex.

His mouth was busy devouring her breasts, and the cowboy hat he was wearing declaring him a rogue Texas Ranger, which happened to be the only thing he was wearing, really did it for me.

Why?

Because the man I happened to have the hots for was also a Texas

Ranger, although he didn't wear his cowboy hat unless he was going to a court appearance or doing something official like serving an arrest warrant.

Wolf didn't like wearing hats.

According to his sister who I'd asked about his choice in uniforms, Wolf didn't like wearing anything that impeded his eyesight.

Personally, I didn't care if he had any problems seeing in his hat.

Wolf in his cowboy hat was devastating.

Not just to my panties, though, but to my heart as well.

Nipples tingling at the sight of the man on the screen penetrating the woman, I shifted my legs and froze when my foot encountered something hard at my back.

Then a hand found my hip, and I gasped, turning over so fast that I hit my head on my unknown bed mate's chin.

The man cursed low and succulently, then rolled and pinned me to the bed, the sheet I was using as a cover pinned so tightly against me that it was nearly impossible to move.

"Oh, my God!" I yelled at Wolf. "What are you doing in my bed?"

He grinned at me.

"An even better question is why are you watching porn alone?" he countered.

My mouth dropped open, and my eyes floated to the left, enabling me to see the TV where cowboy hat dude was drilling his sex partner.

He was fucking her so hard that the office desk they were using was skidding across the floor with each thrust of the man's hips.

The man's gun belt was on the floor around his feet, and his shiny golden badge was winking each time the light hit it as he thrust forward.

"This wasn't on when I went to bed," I lied.

He grinned at me.

"Is that right?" he asked. "You might want to call and contest this with the front desk, then. They'll charge you for it."

He held the phone out to me from the bedside table, and I growled.

"How do you expect me to get it if you're pinning me down?" I asked him.

He moved until I could move my arms, and it was then I realized I was naked.

I certainly hadn't gone to bed naked.

I'd gone to bed with leggings and a t-shirt on.

I'd definitely remember going to bed naked that was for sure.

Wolf's eyes immediately honed in on my bare breast, and he licked his lips.

"What are you doing?" I asked again.

"Something incredibly stupid, apparently."

CHAPTER 10

*Don't let anyone ever treat you like you're a yellow Starburst.
You're a fucking pink, motherfucker! Don't let anyone ever tell you
differently!
-Words of wisdom*

Raven

The moment his mouth descended to my nipple my brain short-circuited.

I'm not talking about forgetting how to speak, either.

I forgot to fucking breathe.

"Take a breath," he whispered as he noticed I wasn't breathing. "This'll work better if you participate."

"I can't move my arms," I informed him.

He grinned, and it was then that I realized that he still had my nipple between his top and bottom teeth.

"You can move if you want to move," he replied as he switched to my other breast.

I moaned as he did, my eyes crossing as he started to suck on my nipples in short, sharp pulls.

Each suck had my body shimmying.

Wolf's eyes were on mine, though, and they were clearly telling me to 'stay still.'

So I chose to stay still, allowing him to do with me what he wanted.

His hand smoothed up my side, and suddenly I found my arm up and over my head as his arm came back down to rest just above the bend of my elbow.

"Keep your arms up high," he ordered me. "I want to suck your pussy."

My mouth dropped open.

"That's not..." he stopped me before I could get the full sentence out of my mouth.

"Shhh," he said. "We're doing this my way, and you'll like it."

When I would've replied to that, too, he stopped playing with my breasts and moved until we were eye level.

"You know."

I feigned innocence.

"I know what?" I asked sweetly. Deviously.

He pushed the sheet down, leaning on one knee to remove it from underneath him before doing the same for the other side.

The moment it was clear of my body, I tried to cover up out of instinct.

He caught my hands before I could make it, and then straddled my waist.

"Keep your hands up here, or I'll have to get creative." Wolf put my hands up where he wanted them, and then let them go.

I immediately grabbed for his hair which was tickling my breasts, sinking my fingers so deep that I thought he'd never pry them loose.

He, however, showed me that he didn't give a shit if it hurt as he pulled my fingers from his hair, and I didn't let up an inch on those luscious locks of black hair.

The moment my fingers were free, he leaned over and grabbed my bra from the bedside table, a place where I wouldn't have put it, and did some maneuvering against the wrought iron headboard.

I started to writhe against him, but he stilled my hips by settling his weight onto me.

"Still," he ordered, moving forward so fast that I jumped.

His eyes came so close to mine that I blinked.

"What are you doing?" I asked, glancing up at what he was doing above my head and then meeting his eyes once again.

"I'm tying you to the bed," he said so casually that my mouth dropped open in surprise.

"You can't do that," I said, yanking my hands down.

"Yes, I can," he showed me by doing just that.

His hands moved like lightning, twirling and circling my hands so fast that I never even saw it coming.

I yanked again and got about an inch of give before the elastic of my bra straps caught and yanked my hands back against the frame where Wolf had tied them.

"Told you to stay still," he muttered. "You want to do this on your back or your knees?"

I blinked.

"What do you mean?" I asked.

"If you don't pick one or the other," he said, getting off of my hips and standing.

My eyes finally chose that moment to take him in.

He wasn't wearing anything truly great, but what he had on, he worked. *Well.*

Faded blue jeans that looked like they would probably be more productive as a dust rag than an article of clothing sat low on his hips. A white t-shirt that was tight as sin and would be indecent on anyone but him.

It was splayed so tightly across his chest that I could make out each tiny bump on his hard nipples.

His pecs stood out starkly against the white fabric.

However, it was the bulge in his jeans that my eyes were drawn to.

His hands came up to smooth down his abs, stopping at the waistband of his jeans to hook into the fabric before he lifted his shirt, and undid his belt.

He carefully laid the belt down, which I now saw had a gun attached to it, onto the floor beside the bed.

The next to go was the t-shirt, which he hooked at the back of the collar.

He then proceeded to do what every hot guy did when they took their shirt off.

Hunching his shoulders, he bent forward and removed the t-shirt, removing first one arm followed shortly by the next.

The t-shirt was thrown onto the floor next to his belt, and I gulped.

"I'm not going to hurt you, Rave," he whispered gruffly.

I licked my lips and finally made my way past his taut abs, taking in his black beard and equally dark hair.

My eyes finally settled on his.

"I know," I cleared my throat. "I'm just taking in the view."

He rolled his eyes, and then my heart rate started to pick up as he reached for the button of his blue jeans.

I licked my lips as he unzipped, and then nearly cried out when he let the jeans hang on his hips before crawling back into the bed with me.

"You're not answering my earlier question," he said as he settled in between my legs.

I widened them as far as I could to allow him access without thinking, then immediately realized what I was doing and tried to close my legs.

He caught both of my thighs with large hands, and pushed them flat to the bed.

My thighs screamed in protest, but the look in Wolf's eyes held no mercy.

"Wolf," I tried to say.

He grinned.

"I'm going to choose since it's obvious that you can't," he said, taking one leg and lifting it up and over his head until my legs were closed.

I started to protest, but before I could even get a word out I was flipped onto my belly, my face going into the bedding with the suddenness of the move.

I tried to push up and move my head out of the cloud like pillows, but before I could find purchase my hands caught on the elastic that was tying them to the frame and I face planted again.

Wolf's hands on my hips had me stilling, and my heart started to hammer in anticipation.

As fully exposed as I was, I should feel more embarrassed.

I wasn't. How could I be when one of the world's sexiest men was touching me? Rubbing his hands up and down my thighs like he wanted nothing more but to feel his skin against mine?

And that was exactly what he was doing.

He was taking his time, getting to know my body with his.

"Your skin is so light compared to mine," he cleared his throat. "I need you to say yes."

"Yes," I said without hesitation.

He chuckled darkly, and then I felt his beard against my backside.

Shivers started to race up my spine and down my legs, following the path his lips were taking up and down my ass.

When that perfect set of lips stopped at the very bottom of my ass, right where all the good stuff started, blood rushed to my face.

His beard was tickling my clit, and I couldn't help but squirm.

He chuckled darkly against my skin, and then his hands started to move further down.

Abruptly, his hands parted my thighs even wider, stealing my breath from my lungs with the suddenness of it.

"I've dreamed of being here, between your legs, for months," he whispered. "Are you sure you're ready for what I'm about to give you?"

I laughed darkly.

"Wolf," I turned my head to the side so he could hear me more clearly.

"I'm not traumatized," I informed him. "I'm so far from traumatized by what those jerkoffs did to me it's not even funny. I'm more traumatized by what they did to July than what they did to me…"

Before I could talk more, he reached up and covered my mouth.

"A yes or no would've been sufficient," he rasped, his finger dipping into my mouth.

With no choice, I sucked his finger into my mouth and nursed on it like it was his cock, my tongue circling around the tip, nipping and swirling.

He abruptly yanked his finger from my mouth.

"Might wanna check that mouth of yours while I eat you," he said. "The neighbors I saw coming in looked like the type to call the staff if you get too loud."

Before I could add a word to the conversation, he flipped to his back and slid between my thighs.

"Sit on my face," he ordered me.

My mouth dropped open and my eyes widened.

"I can't sit on your face. I'm a big boned woman! I'll smother you!" I yelled out, nodding towards my hips for emphasis.

Wolf snorted and shoved my thighs out with the bulk of his arms, forcing me to sit on his face whether I wanted to or not.

My vagina practically landed in his mouth, and his tongue immediately started to assault my clit.

The coarse hair of his beard tickled me along my inner thighs and grated teasingly along every single inch of my pussy.

When his fingers moved, I wasn't expecting it.

I'd gotten so into riding his face, not caring whether or not I was smothering him – surely he'd tap out if I was close to killing him – that I just wasn't prepared.

I honestly had no idea, I was the most inexperienced person in Texas.

What Wolf was doing to me, what I was feeling… the moment his fingers became acquainted with the inside walls of my pussy, I started to come.

And come hard.

One second I was riding the feel-good train, and the next my eyes were crossing in bliss.

I screamed, so loud and long, that Wolf slid up between me and the bed and shut my mouth with his own.

I tasted myself on him, and I started to go wild.

I could smell myself, too. It was an oddly erotic experience, one that I never thought would be as arousing as it was.

The sheer naughtiness of the act had my libido going from rearing-and-ready-to-go to get-inside-me-now.

I broke the kiss to draw in some much-needed oxygen to my brain and stared at him.

"Condom. And untie me," I ordered harshly, panting lightly.

He grinned and released my hands from their bindings. Then he reached for something in his pocket, and I finally realized why the jeans had stayed on.

"Clever man," I said to him. "Now take them off."

He pushed on my belly and I took the hint, giving him room to work the jeans down the long length of his thighs.

His knees bumped into my ass, one at a time, and I groaned as the coarse hair covering his thighs brushed against my still sensitive skin.

Then I felt his hands working between us, all the while his eyes stayed on mine, eyes locked in place.

"More light," I pleaded with him. "I want to see us."

He reached blindly for the light next to the bed and flicked it on, temporarily blinding me as he replaced his hands on my hips.

He tilted his hips, and suddenly the tip of his cock was at my entrance.

After a quick study of my face and my willingness to continue, he started to ease inside.

My mouth dropped open as his length filled me, one delicious thick inch at a time, until he was buried so deep inside of me that I could hardly find any breath to fill my lungs.

Then he bottomed out and I closed my eyes.

"Open them," he ordered. "You wanted to watch. Watch."

I licked my lips, and unintentionally got a taste of Wolf in the process.

His beard tickled my chest and chin, teasing me with multiple sensations so crazy that I couldn't begin to control myself as nearly every synapse I had inside my body started to fire.

"Fuck," I breathed.

Wolf's eyes still held mine, and I wanted to close them so badly it hurt.

But if Wolf wanted me to watch, then I'd watch.

My hands were starting to ache from the force I was using to ride him and pull myself back up, but I roughly shoved it to the back of my mind and got back to more important matters. Such as the way my pussy felt with his huge cock sliding in and out of it at a steady pace.

"So good," I breathed, dropping my mouth for a kiss.

He kissed me back, but yet again, I was the one to end it.

His hands tightened on the expanse of skin where my thighs met my ass, and I had to drop down hastily in order to prevent myself from bucking completely off his cock at the way his strength, so commanding and controlled, felt against my ass.

"Hurry," I whispered, licking my lips once again and barely missing his lip by less than a hairsbreadth.

He didn't hurry, though.

He stayed the same pace the whole time.

In. Out. In. Out.

Long, slow, deliciously deep glides that were making my eyes cross.

I dropped my forehead down to rest on Wolf's, all the strength leaving me as I surrendered to his movements.

And he didn't disappoint. He continued to fill me, so nice and easy, that the build was slow.

My womb was on fire, ramping up my anticipation of the release that was to come.

Wolf's beard continued to tickle my chest as our breath intermingled.

His strong thighs were pushing up while my hips came down as he filled me.

His hands on my hips guided me exactly where he wanted me to go, not letting me deviate from the pace he was setting.

Then I felt his hands clench down tight, and he spoke the first word since we started.

"Dying."

I took that to mean he was close.

Knowing he would come soon, I started to grind my hips, and he allowed it.

The rasp of his pubic hair against my distended clit was exactly what I needed to push me over the edge.

My breath caught.

My skin started to tingle.

My eyes closed until only the barest of slits was left, enabling me to see Wolf's black eyes and nothing else.

I inhaled just as he exhaled, and it was almost as if I stole the breath right out of his lungs.

The orgasm that shook my curvy body was nothing less than spectacular.

One second I was enjoying the burn, and the next I was detonating into a million tiny pieces.

Fragments of my control and Wolf's surrounded us as he lost what little strength he had holding him back, and he started to thrust so hard inside of me that I could do nothing but go along for the ride.

I bit my lip at one point; so hard, in fact, that I could taste blood.

Wolf's mouth met the skin of my throat as he buried his face, wrapping his arms so tightly around me that I let out a shuddering breath.

He grunted as his ab muscles flexed, cock twitching as his release rushed out of his body and into the condom.

For a fleeting moment, I was upset that his release wouldn't be filling me up, but then I quickly dismissed that thought. Now wasn't the time. Neither of us was in the right place now to deal with the repercussions of that one life-changing act.

As our breathing came back to normal, I lifted my hips. Wolf's cock left my body and landed on his belly, and I leaned back down to trap it between us.

It hadn't gone down so much as an inch since he'd come, and I barely contained the urge to smile.

I liked that he wanted me. *Still* wanted me.

I liked it a lot.

It was when I tried to place my hand on Wolf's face that I realized my hands were still tied to my bra. Kind of. It'd broken at some point, and when he released me from the headboard, the thin piece of material that'd broken off the main part of my bra was still dangling from my wrist.

"You're going to have to buy me a new bra," I told him as I untangled my hands and sat up.

Wolf's hands started to roam as I rubbed the circulation back into my hands, and I gave him a glare.

"No," I said. "I'm tired."

He chuckled and rolled.

My back hit the bed and he hiked my hips up wide, grinding his cock into my pussy as he did.

"Don't," I whispered.

He dipped the tip of his cock back inside of me, and my neck arched as my body practically begged to have him back inside.

"Please," I whispered.

I couldn't figure out whether I was asking him to get off of me, or get me off. Regardless, I was ready for him to do something.

He did.

He ripped off the condom and tossed it unceremoniously to the floor beside the bed.

Then he rolled us one last time, and I was now curled into his body, head on his chest. One foot was wrapped around his legs, and one hand was resting high in the middle of his chest. My casted hand was up high between our bodies resting on the pillows.

The position would've been awkward had Wolf not seemed just as sated and comfortable as I was.

I was happy. Comfortable. And oh, so sleepy.

In fact, I was so comfortable and sleepy that I was literally on the verge of falling back asleep when he had to go and open his big mouth.

CHAPTER 11

A lot of people are only alive because I shed too much hair to get away with murder.
-Everyday women problems

Raven

"You'll stay with me," Wolf said abruptly, turning his head to face me.

I shook my head.

"I can't stay with you. I have a couple renting my place right now, but I'll go home as soon as I give them the notice that I promised to give," I said. "And these sheets are so soft."

To prove my point, I rubbed my face in the sheets, and then transferred my face to Wolf's chest.

Wolf's hairy chest.

"The sheets are so much softer," I informed him.

He snorted and pushed me off, picking up the discarded condom from the floor and dropping it in the waste paper basket right next to the desk before heading to the bathroom.

"That's gross," I told him. "You need to take that and wrap it up in some toilet paper. Then flush it."

He shut the door on me and did his business, and I laid back and snuggled into the bed while I waited for him to come back.

I was sexually satisfied, tired, and full.

That was the perfect combination for a full eight hours of sleep, had Wolf let me close my eyes for more than five seconds.

"Do you want to go get breakfast?" he called after I heard the toilet flush.

"No," I murmured, getting more comfortable by reaching for the sheet and pulling it up and over my head.

The light from the nightstand was interrupting my ability to fall asleep.

If I could just get up and block out the light...

"Ack!" I squawked when Wolf fell down onto the bed beside my prone body, propelling me inches into the air before I landed back down in my previous position. "What the hell, man?"

Wolf chuckled as he yanked the sheet away and tossed it to the floor.

"You can sleep in my thousand thread count sheets," he said. "*Later.*"

"I don't want to do it later. I want to do it now. It's still dark out," I informed him, pointing to the windows where there was absolutely no sun shining through the slats of the blinds.

"Those are blackout curtains," he told me, getting up and yanking the window open. "See?"

I flinched at the sun that was peeking up over the clouds, and groaned.

"Please," I whined. "I only need an hour tops."

"It's already seven. I slept beside you for four hours before I woke you. I have to be at the office at nine, and if I hurry I can drop you at my place and we can get breakfast," he said.

"I have to find a job," I told him.

"Come work at the office," he offered. "I need someone to do the filing and answer phones, besides me. You can even bring your dog with you."

I gave him a look, but it was lost on him since he wasn't looking at me.

Instead he was looking down the plane of his chest and belly as he buttoned his jeans.

"I have to suck in when I button my pants," I said.

He looked up and grinned at me but wisely chose not to comment on that statement.

When I reluctantly started to move out of the bed, he leaned one muscled forearm into the bed and leaned over until he could place his mouth on mine.

"What was that for?" I asked breathlessly as he pulled away from me.

My breathing was ragged, and he hadn't done much more than touch his lips to mine.

"I'm happy," he said.

I blinked.

"You're not normally?" I asked carefully.

He shrugged.

"I am and I'm not. My life is one of murder and mayhem. It's nice to have something in it that's soft and understanding, and who likes spending time with me. Oh, and who's over the age of five," he teased.

I reached up and ran the palm of my hand over his beard.

"I can't get enough of you. I lose my mind when you're on top of me, but if we don't hurry, we'll miss breakfast," I whispered.

He leaned down and kissed me one more time, taking me all the way down to the mattress.

His hard body pressed against mine, and it took everything I had in me not to wrap my legs around his waist.

However, he was wearing pants already, and I wasn't sure he'd appreciate wearing a wet spot courtesy of my pussy on his pants while we ate.

The town talked as it was; there was no reason to give them any more ammunition than they already had.

"I'm considering the merits of breakfast," I swallowed. "Are you sure you're hungry?"

He nodded against my lips.

"Yep. Starved. Took me two hours last night to find you when I could've been sleeping beside you," he informed me.

I laughed and rolled until my back was to him.

Standing up, I stretched my arms up high over my head, groaning when all of my sore muscles un-bunched and stretched out.

"Ughhhh," I groaned. "I'm going to be dead by eight o'clock."

Wolf got up and headed for his shirt that was across the room, but his eyes stayed on me.

Well, my breasts, not me in particular.

But I enjoyed it anyway.

"Do I have time to shower?" I asked.

He shook his head.

I rolled my eyes.

"You just want me to smell of you, don't you?" I teased.

His brows rose.

"There something wrong with that?"

I shook my head.

"Not a damn thing."

***

"I was being serious, you know," I told Wolf. "I'm not working for you."

"Just trust me," he said. "You'll understand why I need the help the moment you walk inside, okay?"

Rolling my eyes, I walked in the door that Wolf held open for me, then promptly blushed when I came face to face with Griffin, Wolf's Texas Ranger partner, and another member of the MC that Wolf was a part of.

"Hello, Griffin," I said to the large blonde Viking. "How are you and Lenore doing?"

Griffin grinned, his eyes zeroing in on the hickey on my neck.

"Fuckin' awesome," he replied. "And you?"

I blushed beet red and shrugged. "Been better."

It was true.

I'd tried to sneak around and pay for breakfast with my card earlier at the diner and was promptly told by the waitress that my card had been declined.

I then had to go back to Wolf and tell him what happened.

His face had frozen, and he'd leaned over and withdrawn a couple of twenties from his pocket and placed them both on the table before standing up. Slowly. Then he'd proceeded to take my hand and drag me out of the diner with everyone and their brother watching him do it.

He'd not said a word until we'd pulled into the parking lot of his office, where he proceeded to say that I would be working there and not to argue.

Which led us to now, and my inappropriate attire for a person that was going to work at a law enforcement office.

"Wolf said you were going to file and answer phones. That true?"

I blinked, then nodded my head. "For today, anyway."

A slight grin tugged at the corner of his mouth, and I could suddenly see the hardness of his features melt away into something devastatingly handsome.

"You'll stay if you do a good job today," he responded.

I rolled my eyes and moved out from between the two men, freezing when I saw the state that the office was in.

"This is…disgusting," I told them. "Don't y'all know how to use a trash can?"

Wolf chuckled as he walked in the direction of what I assumed was his desk.

However, there were so many coffee cups, chip bags, candy wrappers and fast food containers that I wasn't sure I would classify it as that.

Then there were the files.

Stacked at least two feet high all the way around the room.

"Where exactly are these file cabinets that you want me to file these in?" I asked the two men.

"In the back room," Griffin said as he passed, heading to his desk, which didn't look much better than Wolf's.

Although it looked like he at least managed to get most of his trash into the large trashcan beside his desk, even if it looked like he hadn't emptied it in weeks.

"Don't y'all have a cleaning crew to do this?" I asked them.

"Don't trust anyone right now," Wolf called. "Come here and let me show you something."

I moved to his desk and stopped beside him.

He was pointing at his computer, and I leaned forward, my breasts brushing his muscled forearm, as I read the email he had pulled up.

"So Travis thinks that you've pissed off someone who's computer savvy?" I surmised once I finished reading. "Why does it have to be someone computer savvy? Why can't he just pay someone to do all this?"

"Because fucking with multiple people's lives, especially the majority of those people being in law enforcement, isn't something that a run-of-the-mill hacker would want to get involved in. Simply being paid wouldn't be enough of an incentive for this."

"True," I allowed. "But what if you pissed the computer person off, too?"

Wolf's lips thinned. "I think it's someone that's connected with the case that I'd been working on before you and my sister got involved. It was a large-scale sex trafficking ring, and they kept their inner circle very small and tight. I made a significant dent in their operation by pinning Jensen and Barrett. I got too close, and now he's warning me to back off by showing me his considerable power and just how far he can reach."

I pursed my lips.

"I don't even know what to say to this," I told him. "I have no intimate knowledge of stuff like this besides what I've read in romance novels."

His lips twitched.

"I'm showing you this because I thought you'd want to read the bottom part," he said, smiling.

His smile was so fucking sexy that I wanted to kiss it off his face, but I could hear Griffin typing away at his computer, so any hanky panky would have to wait until later. Much later.

Wolf's son would be staying with him tonight since it was Friday, and he'd have him all weekend.

"I don't want to work with him," I told Wolf. "He's mean."

Wolf chuckled and pushed my bottom forward.

I took the hint and moved until I could plop down into his lap.

"What's the problem?" Wolf asked softly. "He said you can do this from home. Which means you can do both jobs from here. You'll be getting paid twice. Works out well for both of us, to be honest."

"He fired me. I can't believe he fired me," I said, surprised because it was true. I still couldn't believe he fired me.

I'd come into the office, and he'd called me into his sanctuary where he immediately ripped out my heart by telling me I had to leave. Not just my job, but my home as well.

"He never meant it to be permanent," Wolf said gently. "He wanted you safe, and he can't make you safe without being with you every hour of every day. Something that he just couldn't do."

I pursed my lips and chose not to answer.

That didn't mean much to me. I could've continued to work my job and go home just like I'd been doing. What had changed?

"How do you know all of this?" I asked him suspiciously.

Wolf grinned.

"We talk about you," he said, no apology whatsoever coloring his voice.

I narrowed my eyes.

"Why?" I asked. "Y'all don't even get along."

He nodded his head in agreement.

"We don't," he agreed. "But we're still willing to work together to make sure nothing happens to that pretty little face of yours."

"So you're only with me because of my pretty face?" I asked, fluttering my eyelashes at him.

He rolled his eyes and pushed me off his lap.

I took the hint before he dumped me on the floor and headed to the other side of the desk while he moved his big body around to where Griffin was standing.

He said something to the big man who was on the phone, then headed to the back of the room where he disappeared into the door.

Griffin finished up with his phone call and headed in the same direction.

I leaned my butt against the desk and wondered what I was supposed to do now.

Then my question was answered when the two men came back out with a filing cabinet between them.

Setting it down between the two desks, they turned and disappeared into the next room.

I guess that answered that.

They wanted me to work.

Did I want to work? For Wolf? That seemed like a breach in protocol. There had to be a law somewhere that said a woman who had no clue what the hell she was doing couldn't work for two Texas Rangers without first getting some proper training.

Shouldn't I be sworn in or something? Promise to keep all their secrets or they have the right to remove my tongue from my head?

Obviously there wasn't, because once they got the last of the filing cabinets—eight total—Griffin headed back to his desk while Wolf headed to me. "You're ready to work."

I hid my smile.

"Are you sure I shouldn't be…I don't know… read my rights?" I asked.

He chuckled. "I don't know. Should you?"

I didn't like that smile on his face. The fact that he was laughing at my inner turmoil had my chest expanding and my eyes narrowing as I placed both of my hands on my hips.

"You don't have to make fun of me!" I informed him haughtily.

His grin disappeared. "I'm not making fun of you. I'm wondering what you're holding back from. This is the exact same shit you did at Hail Auto Recovery. Travis said as much."

I sighed.

"I'm nervous. I don't like change," I admitted. "Are you sure you want me here? And in your house? That seems like you'll see me too much."

Wolf snorted.

"I'm in my office about twenty percent of the time, if not less. Usually only for lunch and then I'm gone." He pointed to his desk in an as-you-can-see gesture. "I work about sixty hours a week. You'll be safe here, though. The Uncertain Saints have this office wired, as well as practically the whole block."

He took my hand and led me to the window.

"You're safe going across the street to the diner. You're also safe in Lenore's shop," he pointed to a building down the road.

"Oh," I said. "I didn't realize that she was this close to you," I admitted.

He rumbled in agreement.

"You're also safe at Annie's hair salon there." He pointed at another building next to Lenore's shop.

Relief started to seep into me.

Knowing I wasn't trapped really did a lot for my anxiety level.

"What about when I'm done here and want to go home?" I asked.

"Then I'll take you. Or, if I'm not available, one of the boys." He led me back to his chair. "You can take my desk until we can get you a new one. Sometimes Mig's office is here as well, but his shit's in the backroom so you won't need to touch that area unless he asks you to. Okay?"

I nodded my head.

"Bathroom?" I asked, just thinking of the idea.

"Backroom," he said, pointing at the door across the wide-open room.

While I was looking, he bent down and placed his mouth on mine.

I gasped and he took advantage of the situation, delving his tongue into my mouth.

I lost my balance and ended up on the desk, which he took one step further and leaned me backwards.

Old food bags crunched, and something heavy knocked to the floor by my foot, but I was too lost in that kiss to notice…or care.

When he let me back up for air a few moments later, I gasped and stared up at him in shock.

"You can't do that when we're at work like this!" I hissed, pushing off the desk and away from him.

I looked over to see if Griffin saw but realized that the filing cabinets hid us from his view.

Thank God.

The windows to the outside, however, were open wide.

Anyone who wanted to look in could see.

"Don't do that again," I ordered him.

Wolf's smile was wide, and he shook his head at me.

"If I want to fuck you on that desk with the whole world watching, you'll let me," he taunted me.

My brows likely raised to the roof on that statement.

"What the hell makes you think that?" I crossed my arms over my chest and started to tap my foot.

"Because you can't get enough of me. You like me. You lose your mind when I'm on top of you, my body down the length of yours. You won't be able to help yourself," he teased.

I rolled my eyes.

I'd said those words this morning to him while we'd been fucking.

"I'm going to stay silent during our lovemaking if you don't watch it," I pointed at him for emphasis.

He flashed his white teeth before yanking on my finger that was outstretched toward him.

I went, liking my finger attached to my body, and landed against him with a hard thump.

Breathless from the kiss already, I lost what little I had left and glared.

"I'm going to go to work. If you want food, call the diner. They'll deliver. Tell them to put it on the Rangers' account, *comprende?*"

I gave him a thumbs-up, even though both of my arms were around his back.

"Good."

Then he was gone, Griffin following him a few moments later, leaving me alone in the office staring after them.

CHAPTER 12

Classy as balls.
-T-shirt

Wolf

I wiggled my jaw as I stared at the man on the floor with a look of such disdain that it was a surprise he didn't burst into flames from the scathing look I directed at him.

"Mother fucker," I growled. "What the fuck was that for?"

My head was now pounding, and I hadn't been gone from the office for even fifteen minutes.

That's how long it'd taken me to get a call from Travis and then immediately detour to this little peckerhead's place to find him not only fucking with my life, but fucking with my sister's life.

"You were coming at me like you were about to eviscerate me!" the kid squealed.

"I was," I promised him. "Get the fuck up."

The kid stood from where he'd thrown himself down to protect his head.

From what, I still didn't know.

In his haste to cover said head, he'd fallen and had taken not just the table, but his computer and bookshelf out as well.

In my haste to save the computer from biting the dust, which I did somehow manage to save, I'd gotten a jaw full of keyboard.

"I'm sorry!" he cried.

I looked at the little kid.

"You know you're doing wrong," I surmised. "You know you've been fucking with stuff you shouldn't be."

The kid's eyes filled with tears.

He had to be fifteen at most.

"Yes, Sir," the kid confirmed. "I...I'm sorry."

I crossed my arms over my chest and looked over to Griffin who was standing beside me.

He hadn't moved to do anything as it all went down, so he, of course, was clean of the Coke that'd spilled on the floor, as well as the dozens of powdered donuts that were now soaking up the Coke.

"I don't know," Griffin said. "How old are you, kid?"

The kid bit his lip.

"Fifteen. Sixteen next week," he answered, whisper soft.

I glared at him.

"So you know you've been hacking into DMV records. Bank accounts. Government fucking, blacked out, nobody sees them but God records?" I gave him my best glare, and to be honest, I knew it was chilling.

I knew that the minute I said 'God' that he'd flinch, and he didn't disappoint.

I used to be a drill sergeant in the Marines.

I knew my shit. I knew what to do to get a reaction out of a fucking kid. It didn't matter that this one wasn't eighteen and under my employ.

He was a wayward fucking soul, and no matter what he did to me or my sister, he was still a kid.

A dangerous kid, but a kid nonetheless.

"I'm sorry!" the kid started to wail.

"What's your name?" I asked shortly, fed up with the crying and it'd just begun.

"Xavier," he sniffled.

"Xavier what?" I persisted.

"Xavier Delgado," he answered.

"Where's your parents?"

Griffin stepped around me to pick up the bookshelf that'd tipped over, and I snapped my fingers at Xavier when his eyes went to follow Griffin's movements.

"Focus," I growled.

Xavier's eyes came back to me with a start, and I nearly caved when I saw the fear in his eyes.

He didn't like having Griffin at his back.

His body was tense, and his eyes were hyper aware.

He kept trying to look behind him, and then stopped the moment he realized what he was doing.

"My mom's dead. My father's…gone," he hesitated.

"Gone where?" I pushed.

Xavier bit his lip.

"Xavier," I said shortly. "You're really close to going to jail. In Texas, you can be charged as an adult for crimes such as the ones I know you've committed. Not to mention I haven't even had the chance to go through your computer."

Xavier's head dropped.

"My papa left me. Traded my services to some *gringo* who needed them." He bit his lip. "Everything I've done is what he's forced me to do."

"What 'gringo'?" I asked, sensing that this would be the break I needed.

"Tall. Brown hair. Curly. Crazy eyes that make him look fucking demented." Xavier pointed to his eyes as he gave his colorful explanation.

"Ice blue," I guessed.

Xavier nodded exuberantly. "Yes!"

"Name's Josh Fry?" I continued.

"Don't know his name," Xavier said, his accent getting thicker. "He never gave me a name, and I didn't ask. I get paid once a week. He comes to see what I got accomplished every week, gives me cash and then leaves."

I crossed my arms over my chest.

"You're all alone?" I asked.

He nodded.

"You paying the bills?" I held out my hand.

He took it, hesitantly, and I pulled him to his feet.

"Yes." He licked his lips nervously. "I pay them in person when they're due. Pay in cash."

"You going to school?"

He shook his head.

"No."

"You haven't had a truancy officer here wondering why you're not at school?" The thought that nobody cared about him was starting to tug at my heartstrings.

The kid was fifteen. Still a baby, and all alone in this harsh world that we lived in.

Xavier shook his head no.

"No, Sir."

I looked around at the trailer house.

It was just like the one I'd grown up in with my sister.

Not a surprise considering it was only about seven trailers down from the one where I'd spent the first eighteen years of my life.

I could still practically hear the whispered, cruel words from the town residents when they saw July and me walk into an establishment. Could remember the exact words that I tried to shield July from.

Now those same town residents thought I was a fuckin' hero but still treated my sister like she was the trash of the trailer park.

I made a decision, one that surprised not just Griffin and Xavier, but me as well.

"Get your computer and whatever you need for tonight," I ordered. "If you have anything else that you think will be of use to us, bring that with you, too."

Xavier's eyes went wide.

"Why?"

"Because you're coming home with me."

***

"What the hell, Wolf?" Nancy, Nathan's grandmother, asked as she got out of the car.

I pointed at Xavier. "Stay there."

"Who's that?" Nancy asked as she got Nathan's bag out of the back of the truck.

"That's a kid I found living by himself today," I said. "He's going to be spending the weekend with me until I can find him somewhere to go."

"Oh," Nancy said. "I fed Nathan after I picked him up from school." She handed me a bag of old French fries and nuggets. "I got enough for you, but they're cold now."

I grinned and pulled Nancy into a one-armed hug.

"How're the knees feeling today?" I asked.

Nancy sighed.

"They've been better. I have a doctor's appointment to get a couple of cartilage building shots in them to see if that helps. I have to have three injections before they'll even consider surgical options." She winced when she stepped to the side and hoisted up Nathan's bag.

I took it from her and walked it to my truck, throwing the bag over the side of the bed before turning back to Nancy.

"Let me know if you need me to take you," I told her. "And I want to know how this weekend goes."

Nancy grinned.

"I'll be fine, Wolf," she smiled. "You're such a worrywart."

"I haven't met your new friend who's somehow managed to keep himself hidden every time I try to meet him, so excuse my worry." I pulled her into a short hug.

Nancy giggled.

"You'll like Frank," she promised. "I'll be going to the Texas Rangers' game. Maybe you can watch and see him there."

I snorted and let her go.

"I'll see what I can do," I told her. "Nathan got his medicine already tonight?"

Nancy nodded her head. "He has. I gave it to him before his dinner."

I walked around to the opposite side of Nancy's three quarter ton Dodge and opened the passenger side door.

The first sight of Nathan after such a long time apart hit me straight in the heart just like it always did.

I sure did love the kid like crazy, and it bothered the hell out of me that I needed Nancy's help.

It helped us both out, though.

We both compromised, and the schedule really worked out well for both of us.

Nancy ran a farm outside of the city and had no trouble keeping Nathan during the week. Fridays through Sundays were a problem for her since her work hands had those three days off. Her granddaughter helped her on the weekends, but it was definitely not something she could do with a small child running underfoot.

Hence, why I got him for those three days.

She was just happy that we could work something out.

When Darren had died, I'd been named as Nathan's legal guardian, and since that was what Darren wanted, nobody, not even Nancy, had protested it.

"Daddy," Nathan's sweet, soft voice filled the cab the moment I started to unlatch him from the car seat.

"Hey, boy," I said. "You fell asleep."

"Tired," Nathan muttered, his voice thick with sleep.

I chuckled under my breath and picked him up.

Nathan automatically curled into my chest and wrapped his arms around my neck.

And everything inside me that'd felt unsettled, instantly calmed.

Nancy's eyes were happy as she watched me round the car with Nathan.

"He helped me birth a couple of goat kids today," she smiled. "I remember doing the same thing with Darren. I definitely wore his little hiney out."

I laughed.

"I was there enough with Darren when goats were born. That is tough work, even if you're only watching," I told her, remembering my own experiences.

Goats were cool and all, but they were a hell of a lot of work, and although I had the land for them at my house, I wasn't ever going to have animals there. Even if they would help me get a tax write off on the land.

"It wasn't that bad," Nancy laughed as she went to the passenger side door of my truck and closed it.

"No," I agreed. "But it sucked."

Nancy laughed, and continued to laugh about the situation until I waved goodbye to her and pulled out of the parking lot five minutes later.

My first time seeing a goat birthed had traumatized me, and it tickled the hell out of Nancy to know that I got squeamish when it came to birthings of any kind.

I'd, of course, thrown up the moment I'd seen the hooves coming out of the goat's vagina and that gave Darren material to rag on me for years to come.

He was also with me the first time I'd witnessed a woman giving birth while on patrol during our deployment in Iraq. I'd thrown up then, too.

And Darren had promptly told his mother. Again.

"This kid doesn't look like he's yours," Xavier observed as we pulled out of the parking lot.

"That's 'cause he's not," I said. "He was my best friend's son. When my best friend died, I was given custody of him."

Xavier made a humming noise under his breath, and stared straight forward, not saying a word, for the remainder of the drive.

The moment I pulled into the driveway of my place, Raven opened the door, and her eyes took in everything at once.

She came to Nathan's side and opened the door as I got out, followed shortly by Xavier.

"Sleepy boy," Raven said as she got Nathan out of his car seat and pulled him into her arms.

I nearly laughed at the sight.

Nathan, at five years old, was almost her height. His feet hung past her knees, and his head was nearly as big as hers.

Did she care that he was practically as big as her? Hell no.

She loved Nathan and had since the moment they'd met.

Two wounded souls always gravitated towards each other, and Nathan was definitely a wounded soul.

Although he'd been given everything he could possibly want in life, he'd had a tough time of it.

When he was only a year old, the man who had shot his father and mother had shot him as well.

He'd taken a bullet to the head and had to have fifteen surgeries to repair the damage.

Although he was okay now, it was touch and go at first, and it'd been a very long road to recovery.

Seeing the two of them together again had my heart fucking pounding for a different reason than had been normal for me lately.

"She the baby mama?" Xavier asked as Raven turned around and walked inside.

"No," I grunted and pushed Xavier. "Get inside."

Xavier reluctantly followed me inside. As he took in my house, I couldn't help but notice that his eyes were haunted, too.

Leaving me to wonder what exactly I thought I could fix with this kid when I couldn't even fix myself.

CHAPTER 13

Of course I'm an organ donor. Who wouldn't want a piece of this?
-Raven's secret thoughts

Raven

"Why are we watching the baseball game when soccer is on?" Xavier asked.

"Because I want to watch the baseball game, and it's my fuckin' TV," I told the annoying kid. "Why don't you go watch your precious soccer on the TV in the room I gave you?"

Xavier grinned.

"I like baseball, too."

Wolf held his hand out for the computer, and Xavier grimaced before giving it to Wolf.

I wanted to laugh.

The two men were very alike, and the fact that they'd just met less than three days ago was telling.

"Nathan," Wolf called. "Your grandma will be here in less than twenty minutes. Are you ready to go?"

Nathan started stomping down the hallway, and I looked up and watched as he made his way toward us dragging his R2D2 rolling bag down the hallway in his wake.

"Dad," Nathan growled. "I can't find Chewy."

I got up and immediately walked to the last place I'd seen his Chewbacca figurine, and immediately cried out in excitement. "Found it!"

Nathan came clomping in with his two-sizes-too-big boots that he just had to have and held his hands out for the tiny figure.

"Where'd you find it, Rave?" Nathan asked, throwing himself at my thighs.

I rocked back on my heels, thankful as hell I had the table at my back.

"On the hutch next to the cars you lined up. And I'm glad Marky Mark didn't find it first," I pointed to the make-shift garage he'd been using as his Hot Wheels' storage facility.

Nathan followed my hand and nodded.

"Those better be there when I get back," he said, pointing at me for good measure.

I held my hand up in a 'I promise' gesture and tried not to break out in a smile.

"Good woman," Nathan said, sounding like he was Wolf's age of thirty-five rather than his actual age of five.

"Dad!" Nathan cried as he walked out of the room, shoving Chewy into his pocket as he went. "Make sure you don't let any girls play with my cars!"

I nearly laughed my butt off, but managed to withhold it. Although, that was only because the doorbell rang, detouring my path to the front door instead of standing at Nathan's back listening to him tell his father about why girls shouldn't be able to play with cars.

"Hi!" I said to the older woman. "You must be Nancy."

The woman's face, very pretty for an older woman, stared curiously at me for long moments before her face split into a grin.

"You look like a fairy princess," the woman replied to my greeting.

"She's an evil fairy princess," Nathan muttered as he walked past us towards the stairs.

Wolf caught up with him before he could even make it to the steps and scooped him up into his arms, tossing him over his shoulders.

"*Daaaddddy!*" Nathan squealed. "I'm going to barf!"

Wolf ignored him and continued to swing them in circles.

I was dizzy just watching them.

A chuckle had me bringing my gaze back to Nancy.

She was watching me watch Nathan and Wolf.

Her eyes filled with something I couldn't quite decipher.

I turned away from the scene outside and continued to get to know Nancy. "I made him eat his vegetables," I explained. "He didn't want to eat the asparagus, but I told him if he didn't eat it, he couldn't have any of the chocolate cake I made."

Nancy grinned.

"My granddaughter and Nathan get the same treatment at my home," she smiled. "Although Nathan's a lot more receptive to vegetables than Iona is."

I leaned against the door frame. "How old is Iona?"

"Twenty-four." Nancy continued on describing her obviously loved granddaughter.

I started to chuckle. "No," I agreed. "I don't think she would be very accepting of her grandmother telling her how to eat at twenty-four."

Nancy grinned. "My house, my rules."

We continued to visit until Wolf came up behind us. "Doesn't Iona pay for groceries, utilities and the car insurance?" Wolf asked, scaring us both.

Nathan was asleep against his shoulder, and yet again I was surprised by the fact.

I'd found over the last weekend, though, that Nathan could sleep still anywhere and everywhere.

Not much had changed on that front in the months since I'd first met him.

"I still own the house," Nancy said somewhat defensively. "She's more than welcome to leave."

I looked to Wolf and immediately had to cover up a choking laugh as I saw him roll his eyes so far heavenward.

"You know Iona will never leave you," Wolf grinned. "But let's go. If I hurry, I can get dressed in some different clothes before I leave for work."

I looked over to Wolf.

He was dirty.

How had he gotten so freakin' dirty?

Wolf caught me studying him and immediately became enthralled in the conversation he was having with Nancy.

I could tell something was wrong, though, especially with the way his eyes seem to light with an inner fire. Or possibly the way he scanned the nearly deserted neighborhood.

The only person doing anything on the entire block was a woman four houses down smoking a cigarette and speaking to someone on her cell phone while she pushed a lawnmower around almost as an afterthought.

"Let's go, Nancy," Wolf ordered, holding his arm out like the gentleman he was.

I backed into the doorway and stared at the dark night waiting for Wolf to come back.

It didn't take him long.

Maybe four minutes tops.

However, the moment he came back around the bend of the house, I knew something was really wrong.

"Wolf," I said, moving forward.

"Inside," he snapped.

My brows rose, but I backed up and moved until he could get inside, which he did moments later.

He slammed the door shut and turned to survey the room.

"Xavier," Wolf called.

Xavier's head, which had been resting on the couch, jerked sideways.

"What?" he asked, standing up slightly.

"Pull up the video feed for the house," Wolf ordered, threading the chain through the holder before backing away and heading toward the living room where Xavier was seated.

"What angle do you want?" Xavier asked.

"Back porch near the driveway," Wolf said in anger.

I watched in fascination as the cameras pulled up on Xavier's small computer screen and then started to replay the last ten minutes.

"Holy shit!" I cried, leaning forward over Xavier's shoulder. "What the fuck was that?"

"That," Wolf said, crossing his arms over his chest, "was someone trying to kill me."

"Where is the body now?" I whispered worriedly as he dragged the man to where the trashcans were in a small enclosure on the side of Wolf's house.

The moment he passed behind the trashcans, we lost the angle, only for it to appear five seconds later, from a completely new angle.

"Chained up on the water faucet," he replied, taking his phone out of his pocket.

"That his foot?" I asked, pointing at the screen.

It was the only thing I could see poking out of the portioned off area.

"Yep," Wolf confirmed, then held up a finger for me to hold on and not speak. "Ridley. Got a trespasser. Tried to hurt my boy … Yes."

My brows rose.

Had the man tried to hurt Nathan?

Now I could see why he'd be mad. Enraged even.

***

"Where are we going?" I asked Wolf for a tenth time, dipping a finger into the cast that was really starting to get on my damn nerves.

It itched like crazy. It never fucking stopped itching.

"Clubhouse," he answered distractedly.

I sighed.

I'd gotten the same answer five times now, and I was getting quite annoyed by his one word answers.

"Why?" I pushed.

"Because Xavier needs to stay somewhere that we're not. We're fucking screwed if everyone gets taken out at the same time. No witnesses, nothing," Wolf explained patiently.

I rolled my eyes.

"Dramatic much?" I teased.

Wolf's eyes were serious when they turned to me.

"We're all likely going to be giving testimonies on the stand that explains what we've all been going through the last month," Wolf said. "How fucking convenient if he took all three of us out at the same damn time."

I looked over at the sleeping Xavier. "I think Peek might kill him."

Wolf snorted and shifted down into third, making me jump when he copped a feel.

"You're doing it on purpose, aren't you?" I asked him.

"He might want to," Wolf said, ignoring my question. "But Alison won't let him. They've never been able to have kids, and Alison does everything she can to live vicariously through the members of the club who have babies."

"She's the one who introduced me to Nathan," I reminded him. "I know how much she wants babies."

"Don't mention that in front of Peek," Wolf muttered as he took the final turn that would lead us to the clubhouse.

A strong bump had something solid in the truck bouncing, and then a low moan followed the thump.

"What was that?" I asked in confusion, looking behind us.

"Did you call your credit card company this morning?" Wolf asked, distracting me from the sound.

"Yeah," I sighed. "Card is now canceled. As well as my debit card, and all of my checks. The account is frozen, so they can't access it anymore, and when I'm ready, I'll start a new one."

I'd found out earlier that morning that someone had charged nearly fifteen grand on my credit card.

When the bank noticed the charges, they deemed it suspicious and called to see if I had made the purchases.

I, of course, hadn't been. So that started a series of telephone calls to everyone and their brother about canceling cards and closing out accounts.

Now the only thing left to my name that wasn't frozen in my account was five hundred dollars that was burning a hole in my pocket.

Cash always had that effect on me.

If that same cash was in my bank account, it wouldn't affect me at all.

The fact that it was sitting in my wallet made me think of going to the store and spending every single bit of it on three hundred bags of Reese's Peanut Butter Cups.

I never said my mind was logical.

He pulled up to stop at the same flat bottom boat that he'd used a few days ago, and I stared.

"The water's gotten higher," I muttered.

"Supposed to go up a few more feet before it crests," Wolf agreed. "Fucking terrible, isn't it?"

I nodded forlornly and got out, being sure to shake Xavier awake as I moved.

Xavier folded his lean body out of the seat and stood beside the truck, staring at the water in front of him.

"This is eerie as fuck," he said, looking at the entire area much the same as I'd done a few days prior.

"It is," I agreed. "We have to take that to the front steps."

I pointed at the flat bottom, and Xavier actually grinned. "Never been on a boat before."

I snorted and walked over to it, stepping inside and taking a seat as I waited for the men to gather bags and computers.

For a fifteen-year-old boy, Xavier sure was concerned about his appearance.

Was that normal for a kid his age?

I wouldn't really know.

I hadn't been around a lot of fifteen-year-old boys.

Oh, my God!" Xavier said once we arrived inside the clubhouse five minutes later. "What is that smell?"

My stomach growled at the smell as well, and I followed my nose to find Alison in the kitchen with a wooden spoon in her hand.

"Lasagna?" I asked hopefully.

I loved lasagna. It was my favorite.

I could eat it seven days a week and twice on Sunday.

However, I valued the clothes that fit over my ass, so it wasn't something I let myself cave on.

Alison turned and smiled.

"Yes," her eyes went to Xavier. "You the boy that fucked with my bank account?"

Xavier's eyes widened.

I grinned.

Wolf and I had been over Xavier's role in all of this the first day he'd been at the house, and it hadn't taken me long to forgive Xavier.

Xavier was fifteen-years-old, but he was a young fifteen. He was an introvert and looked like he rarely had any adult interaction of any kind. And if he did happen to get some adult interaction, it was with a couple of men—his father and a man who forced him to do illegal things—and they weren't what I would call good role models.

"Yes, Ma'am," Xavier replied, his eyes staying straight on Alison's.

Impressed that he was able to hold the older woman's eyes without flinching, I threw my arm over Xavier's shoulder and stared at Alison.

"He's already promised to set everything right, and he's officially switched to the good side," I told her, pulling Xavier down to my level so I could put my head against his.

Xavier took the manhandling like a pro and kept his head pressed to mine while Alison decided what to say or do next.

In the end, she surprised me and went back to cooking without another word.

"I'm going to have a word with Peek," Wolf said. "Then we can go."

I nodded my head and watched him leave, all the while keeping Xavier in a hunched over position.

"You can let him go now, dear," Alison said without turning around.

"She has eyes in the back of her head," I whispered to Xavier. "Don't do anything stupid."

Alison chuckled.

"I heard that."

"She has ears like a hawk, as well," I told him. "One time, when I was staying here while I testified in the case against the men who hurt my friend, she caught me sneaking out of my protective custody. I felt like I was sixteen again."

"Why were you sneaking out?" Xavier asked. "Everybody knows when you sneak out, you get caught."

I rolled my eyes.

"I was a sheltered child. Sort of. More like uncared for. Nobody gave a shit if I snuck out; meaning, at the time, I didn't realize anyone would give a shit that I was leaving," I informed him haughtily.

Xavier smirked and I pushed him away with a hand on his forehead before walking to the bar and planting my ass on the barstool closest to Alison.

Wolf had gone down the hallway to his room or possibly the meeting room, church. Two other people shared that hallway with him, but I couldn't tell you who. The only person that ever interested me in the entire situation was Wolf, and I could tell you just about anything you wanted to know about him.

His height, which was six foot three. His weight, which I happened to figure out only because I asked him a few days ago. His alma mater— LSU. His military occupation. You name it, I knew it.

Wolf had interested me for a long damn time, and I was on top of the fucking world.

My bank account was frozen. I had no health insurance. My dog was being passed around to friends and acquaintances. My car was taking up space in front of an apartment that I was no longer welcome in, and I was unemployed...sort of.

All of that didn't matter, however, with Wolf in the picture.

Wolf had been my dream come true—the one thing I never thought I'd be able to have.

In fact, it still didn't seem real.

Which might explain why I said what I said next.

"Xavier," I said, turning my head to the boy that was still standing where

I'd left him. "Would you mind going to find your room? It's on the right hallway—first room on the right."

Xavier nodded and bolted, not sparing even a 'thank you' or 'okay' before he was gone.

"Interesting kid," Alison said as soon as he left the room. "What was that look you gave him before he left?"

I stared at Alison's back, wondering how in the hell she'd seen the look when she'd been facing the pot at the stove.

Either the woman had exceptional ESP, or she could see out of the sides of her eyes better than the rest of the normal human population.

"I need to talk to you," I hesitated. "I need to talk to someone that's not going to bullshit an answer just to make me happy."

Alison turned her head to stare at me. "And you think I'm that person?"

I nodded my head.

"I do," I confirmed.

Alison smirked.

See, the thing about the woman standing in front of me, was that her husband always came first.

The Uncertain Saints came second, and everybody else came third.

She was a mother hen, and all of the men were her chicks.

If one was in trouble, she was going to be there to help them in any way she could if they needed it.

Right now, though, I was about to ask her something that would go against the grain.

Hell, it went against my grain.

But I needed to do it. I needed to be independent.

I needed to leave, and I needed to do it now before anything more would tie me to this place and to Wolf. I wasn't becoming one of his responsibilities. I wanted to be his partner, not his charity case.

"I need your advice," I murmured, looking over my shoulder covertly to make sure we were alone.

"My advice on what?" Alison asked, giving me her full attention.

I raised my casted hand and scratched my nose.

"You're not going to like it."

Lani Lynn Vale

CHAPTER 14

At my funeral I would like there to be a piñata so they can be happy. But not too happy. To ensure that, I want the piñata to be filled with bees.
-Meme

Wolf

"What is that supposed to be?" Peek asked, looking down at the man who'd been in my truck's bed for twenty-four hours straight now.

Lucky for me, but bad for him, I'd thrown him down on top of the tarp before I'd tied him down to the bed.

I didn't want his piss and shit all over the bed of my truck. I sure as fuck didn't need his blood, either.

The piss he'd relieved himself of was pooling in a wet puddle around the entire length of his body, and if the strained look on his face was anything to go by, he likely had to relieve himself further…and not just of piss.

"How do you like having piss in your hair?" Peek asked the man, prodding him with the shovel that I had in the back of the truck. "Do you want to stay there until you die of dehydration, or would you like to start fucking talking?"

The man tightened his lips even further.

It wasn't until I lost patience and picked up the shovel that he finally started to look afraid…as he should be.

"Tell me now, or I'll relieve you of a kneecap," I said through clenched teeth.

Peek's hand came down on my shoulder, but with the man deliberately spitting at me, the large wad of spit barely missing me, I realized then that whatever tactic we were hoping to employ weren't going to work on this man.

He needed a much more succinct understanding of what would happen if he didn't cooperate.

Hurtling myself up over the edge of the truck, I took the shovel in two hands and swiftly brought the flat part of it down on the man's kneecap.

It broke with a loud pop, and I was left wondering just how loud he could scream with the gag on.

The instant the heavy metal of the shovel met with the guy's kneecap, the bone shattered, and he writhed in pain.

"Gross," Mig said. "He's sloshing his piss all over the bed of your truck."

Mig took a step back, and I went back around the side of the truck, accidentally stepping on the man's hand as I made it over to where I could jump down out of the truck.

The man rolled and tried to take me out at the knees. And he would have, had I been someone else who was not aware of what a guy like him, a guy in his position, might do.

I wasn't stupid, and I sure as hell wasn't born yesterday. I know when someone's being deliberately quiet to try and buy time.

This guy, though, was a fuckin' pro.

It amazed me that he'd been able to lie still and wait for his chance.

Using the shovel as leverage, I lifted my feet and kicked out, knocking the man in the jaw with one booted foot.

I pulled the kick at the last moment, being sure not to knock him out completely. I only wanted to stun him. To let him know that this shit was serious business.

"You look like you're a little too pissed to handle this right now, Wolf," Peek supplied.

I shot him a look and straightened.

Then, without removing my eyes from Peek's, I slammed the flat blade of the shovel against the man's knee.

The man screamed and started to vomit, his gag keeping most of it inside.

"You might want to swallow that so you don't aspirate it," I offered the man my thoughts. "Can't have you dying just yet."

"He's pretty fuckin' good at taking this torture he's been given over the last hour," Griffin said as he arrived at the party. "And you haven't gotten him to say a damn thing?"

I shook my head. "Not one single thing. He's closed up tight."

Sirens started from a far distance away, and I grinned.

Taking one last look at the man, I reared back and brought my steel-toed boot to his temple, knocking him out completely. Likely for quite a while.

"What was that for?" Ridley yawned, seemingly uninterested in the happenings here.

"What's up with you?" I asked him.

"The woman's keeping me up with her barfing," he yawned. "Couldn't fucking sleep a goddamn wink with her moaning."

We all stared at Ridley like he'd grown a second head.

"Your woman's pregnant," I finally said. "What exactly did you expect to happen?"

Ridley shrugged.

"I don't know," he admitted. "I thought it would be an easy pregnancy. Not...this," he settled with. "It's... it's... this is fucking exhausting."

Every last one of us started to laugh.

Jumping out of the truck, I pulled the rolled up bed cover down from the back of the cab, and rolled it all the way down until it covered the entirety of the cab and all its contents, including the now unconscious man.

I'd just locked it with a key that I then gave to Peek when the first police car arrived on scene.

"Unmarked," Ridley observed as he watched the cars pull up to the very back of the truck and stop within a few inches of taking us out.

None of us moved.

Not one of us.

I'd just decided that maybe these fuckers in their unmarked cars needed a little driving lesson when the man I'd been wondering about folded out of the car.

Crazy eyes like Xavier described and all.

"You have one of our agents," the man said with such disdain that I had to check the urge to smile.

"Not sure what you're talking about," I said, standing up straight from my position of leaning against the truck.

The man's eyes narrowed.

"Can I help you?" Ridley asked, pulling his sheriff's hat on and walking toward the man.

"No," the man said.

"Well then, I'm going to have to ask you to leave. This is private property," Ridley's authoritative voice brooked no room for argument, and I had to bite the inside of my lip to keep the laugh from bursting free of my lungs.

I looked around at the parking lot we were standing in.

Sure, it was outside the clubhouse, but it was still off of a public street and everybody knew it.

The man's temper started to fray.

"I'm missing an agent," he said. "And you're fucking with my investigation."

"Then I'll have to be informed of who it is you're looking for, as well as what investigation you're working on," Ridley said pleasantly.

Griffin took his hat off his head, forked his fingers through his hair so it lay flat, and then replaced the hat.

The movement wasn't one of nervousness. No, it was one of effectiveness and knowing when a situation is about to turn bad.

The move had Griffin's hands free of the truck, and now where they were resting on his hips, mere inches away from the gun at his side rather than on top of the truck where any swift movement would be immediately noticed.

Mig and I did much the same, positioning ourselves so that we not only had each other's backs, but so that we also had access to our side arms as well.

"Josh," another man came out from behind the man. "Our GPS tracking info has the beacon within a mile of this address."

"Josh Fry, is it?" I asked with a deceptive calm.

Fry smiled.

"Agent Josh Fry. FBI," he didn't offer his hand and neither did I.

"Interesting," I said, crossing my arms behind my back. "How's it going?"

Josh Fry gave me a look that clearly suggested what he thought of my ridiculous question.

I'd only learned just today that this Josh Fry man was an agent for the FBI.

I'd also learned today that he's served four years in the Army including a tour of duty in Iraq. I'd also learned that none other than Jensen, the man responsible for making Raven's life a living hell for months on end, had been there with him during his brief military career. How convenient for them.

"What are you doing here, Agent Fry?" Ridley asked again, cutting into my thoughts.

Thankfully.

Who the hell knew where those thoughts would have led had I not been interrupted.

"I'm in the middle of a classified investigation, and I need my agent back," he said, not giving us a thing. "He's been missing for a little over 24 hours."

"Interesting," I found myself saying.

The man's eyes cut to me, and I could actually feel the anger brewing in those freakishly odd eyes.

"What's interesting?" the man snapped.

"It's interesting that this supposedly missing man's GPS is leading you to private land," I said conversationally, my eyes focusing solely on the lying piece of shit in front of me.

Luckily, the man currently occupying the bed of my truck didn't seem to want to hurt Nathan—at least not too much—and that proved to be his fatal mistake.

At the time, Nathan had been my main concern. My mind was solely focused on protecting my son, and nothing else.

I pushed Nathan underneath the truck, forcefully telling him to stay put as I also rolled under it and over to the other side, taking the man out with a brutal kick to the ankle that had broken it.

With the guy now down, I delivered a roundhouse kick to his face that knocked him out. Then I was able to pull Nathan out from under the truck and rock him until he fell asleep.

"Funny," Agent Fry said, a sickeningly sweet hint to his voice that set my teeth on edge. "The last time I studied a map of this area, this road leads to a public boat ramp. So there's a lot of traffic. Seems to me, if he was just taking a look-see at the lake, it would be fair of him to be on this road."

He was right.

The road was a cut through to the public boat ramp. But, with all of the flooding, the boat ramp was under water and most of the parking lot was also.

I gritted my teeth and brought my hand up to my face to scratch my beard, my eyes studying the man and his goons at his back.

Xavier's description of the man paying him to hack into everyone's lives fit this guy to a T. Sharp angular cheekbones, curly brown hair, freakishly blue eyes. About five foot ten with his boots on…with them off he'd be about five eight.

The goon at his side looked more authoritative than he did, and I knew in that instant that Josh Fry had a bigger enemy than me.

The man at his side wasn't even trying to hide it.

He wanted me to know that I had an ally on the inside.

His fingers flashed at his side. Fist. Two fingers. One finger. Fist. Fist.

I moved my gaze back to Fry and nodded.

His hand flashed again, and I clenched my fist.

He wanted to meet tonight at 2100. Nine O'clock.

I didn't worry about where. I knew he'd find me.

"I'll need to search the property to find my man," Fry continued, not knowing that something pivotal had just happened. "Don't make me get a warrant."

"You're getting a warrant to search," I told him bluntly. "I know how your kind operates."

Fry's face darkened.

I smiled.

"Fine," he said, crossing his arms. "We'll get our warrant."

Yeah, he would. He'd be back.

There'd be no sign of his agent here, though, when he returned with said search warrant.

CHAPTER 15

I have a pretty big ass, so when I half-ass something, you're still getting something fairly impressive.
-E-card

Raven

"Raven!" Wolf yelled the moment I heard him cross the threshold of his office.

I popped my head out from around the filing cabinet, a thick stack of files in my arms, and stared at him.

"Yeah?" I asked warily, before going back to the filing and trying for all I was worth to act like I wasn't affected by his nearness.

"I need a file on...," he pursed his lips. "Never mind. I'm going to have to call Travis."

He disappeared around the corner, not saying a damn word about the state of the office.

Hell.

Even Griffin had said something.

Immediately.

Twenty minutes ago when Griffin had walked into the office, he took a short pause to look around, nodded his head, and then said, "Good job."

It hadn't been much, but I'd known it was a lot for him.

Wolf, however, had been the man sleeping with me.

And I say 'had' intentionally.

I fully intended not to sleep with him again, but I had a feeling if Wolf made any sort of move on me within the next couple of hours, I'd take him inside of me again without hesitation.

That didn't mean I wasn't still mad at him.

"Gotta go," Wolf said. "You want me to get anything from your apartment?"

I shook my head.

I had everything from my old apartment.

"No," I said softly. "Thank you, though."

He started forward until his face was only inches away from mine.

"If you change your mind, text me," he ordered. "Don't leave by yourself, and try to get the files on top of my desk done before you leave. Leave the bottom one."

Then he was gone, leaving me alone. Again.

"I'm not a fucking charity case," I mumbled as I watched Wolf walk away. "I'm so sick and tired of depending on people to take care of me."

I muttered that statement to Wolf's back as he walked hastily to his truck, not looking back to see if I followed his orders or not.

Walking over to Wolf's desk, I picked up all the files that were on his desk but the last one, filed them, and then walked back to the file I'd left there. Marky Mark followed me and curled up at my feet.

It looked innocuous from the outside.

It was on the inside that really chapped my ass, though.

I pulled the file that was labeled as 'brunette- 28' into my hands and stared at it with disgust.

My whole life was in that folder.

Everything there was to know about me was right there, including the last few months of my life.

The address of Hail Auto Recovery.

A receipt for my fucking dog, along with his picture, that dispelled any hope that I had that Wolf wasn't behind my 'finding' Marky Mark in my yard that day.

Then there was the last known address that put me above the garage of Hail Auto Recovery.

Seeing me had been no accident on Wolf's part. It had all been intentional.

Every last single bit of it.

The amount of money Wolf has spent over the last week taking care of me stared at me in mocking disappointment.

I'd found the folder yesterday during my filing.

I was lucky I happened to read it.

I hadn't read any of the other files.

This one, though, had been thick and large.

Although it'd intrigued me, sitting on the corner of Wolf's desk at the very bottom of a stack of files, I'd intended to put it back into the filing cabinet like I'd done all the rest.

Then I'd bumped the desk with my hip and the file had started to lean over the edge.

A single paper had fallen out, and it had been intriguing enough for me to break my rules and open the folder.

But it was what I'd seen inside that had really floored me.

The first paper had been a picture of Marky Mark.

The second had been all my life's work, starting at when I'd gotten my first job at sixteen, and finishing at my current job at Hail Auto Recovery.

Or my former job anyway.

I'd debated on whether or not to call Travis and ask him to help me, but he'd already told me his thoughts on Wolf. He'd told me that if I chose Wolf, I would have Wolf and not him to count on.

At the time, it'd been saddening, but it'd been Wolf. I knew Wolf.

Or at least I thought I did.

Now I wasn't sure who he was or what I knew… except for one thing.

I needed to get the hell out of Texas.

I was thinking Alaska.

Or Seattle.

A horn honked outside, reminding me that I had less than ten minutes before my ride arrived.

"Shit," I said, as I walked to the window.

Alison waved at me from out by the curb, and I took that as my chance to get the hell out of there.

Since I didn't have a key, I locked the front door from the inside, walked through to the rear of the building and then pushed open the back door. I was leaving my dog in the building. Alison was sending someone over to get him and take him to Wolf's house. It was his dog anyway.

My stuff was exactly where I left it, and I picked up the large beach bag I used for dirty laundry and tossed it over my shoulder.

Grabbing the rolling suitcase I'd purchased at Goodwill, I hurried to the side of the building and ran smack dab into a hard brick wall.

"Oomph," I said, backing up to look at the man I'd walked into.

"Oh," I said. "I'm sorry, are you okay?"

The man smiled, flashing me an exceptionally straight row of white teeth.

"Perfectly fine, darlin'," he said, not waiting for me to respond. "Where's Wolf?"

My lips twisted. "Wolf's visiting a friend right now."

"Okay," he said, looking down at my bag. "You need help with that?"

The man's dark black eyes seemed to sparkle the longer I stood there staring at him like an idiot, but I couldn't make my mind work right.

The man, the handsome devil, was incredibly good looking.

He was tall with black hair, silky and shiny that any lady would've paid a fortune to get.

His mouth was lush and plump.

I smiled at him.

He was a handsome devil, I'd give him that.

He wasn't Wolf, though.

Where this man was calm, Wolf was intense.

When I was around Wolf, I felt like I was revolving around a Wolf vortex. I was unable to do anything without first being sure of where Wolf was.

"No," I finally answered. "I don't need help. Excuse me."

The man moved to the side and I walked in front of him out of the alley.

I wasn't sure what it was about the man, but I instinctively knew he wouldn't hurt me. He reminded me of someone. It was something about his eyes, so much like mine, that made me feel comfortable with giving him my back.

Sure, it was stupid.

A woman in a quickly darkening alley should be vigilant about men at her back, especially ones she met in said dark alley. However, I decided to run with my instincts, and let him follow me out.

I waved when I saw Alison, speeding my steps up before I lost my nerve.

She got out and opened up the back hatch of the Tahoe she was in and stared at me as I hauled my bags into the back.

"You sure about this?" Alison asked. "I'm going to get in so much trouble doing this for you."

I smiled over at her.

"I'm thinking that husband of yours wouldn't allow you to get in trouble," I teased.

Her mouth thinned. "If I didn't agree with why you're doing this, I would say no. I don't want to get involved, but the picture you painted last night was enough to give me nightmares."

I agreed.

Last night, when I was explaining what I wanted, she refused. Vehemently. At first.

Then I told her about my life. About how no matter what happened, it always seemed that other people were taking care of me.

I hadn't lied to her at all.

I'd told her about my parents. My life. How Wolf had found me when he'd gone in and saved his sister.

"Who was that?" Alison asked as I felt, more than saw, the man in the alley move away from our huddle.

"I don't know," I replied. "Someone that was in the back of the alley when I came out. Maybe he works next door."

The door next to Griffin and Wolf's was a body shop that'd just moved in, according to Wolf.

I'd seen quite a few men in and out of the building all afternoon while I waited for Alison to arrive.

I'd been amazed at how much Wolf knew about the men.

"They're in my town," he'd said. *"How could I not know anything about them?"*

Then a disturbing thought occurred to me.

Wolf and I had been in the same city as we grew up.

Karnack was a small town, and it wasn't often that an officer got shot there along with his wife and unborn child.

I'd known a little bit about Wolf before I'd met him, but certainly the bulk of information I'd learned over the time I'd spent with him.

So if I knew anything at all about him from our time in Karnack before we'd actually met, of course he *had* to know about me.

Had to know every single embarrassing detail of my life. Of my childhood.

He had to know how much I hated my life and how badly I had wanted to get out.

In the end, it hadn't been enough, and I'd paid the price for the decisions I made in my attempt to leave there.

I replayed it over and over again in my dreams, and at that moment, I realized that Wolf was hiding more than he should.

"Can we just go?" I asked hastily, now not willing to waste time.

Before, I'd admit, I'd been secretly hoping that Wolf would stop me from leaving.

Now, though, I knew better.

Wolf wouldn't be stopping me from leaving. I was leaving, and there was no one that would stop me.

By the time we arrived at the bus station three towns over, I'd worked myself up into a fine dither.

Alison, though, either didn't notice or didn't care.

Calmly, she pulled up to the curb, hopped out while leaving her car running and had my bags unloaded before I'd made it out of the truck.

"If you need me, you call. No matter what," she ordered.

I smiled.

"I can do that," I told her.

Then, with one last hug, I was alone at the bus station.

No one to blame but myself.

CHAPTER 16

*People say that love is the best feeling, but I think finding a toilet
when you have diarrhea is better.*
-E-card

Wolf

My heart was in my throat.

As I made my way to the last room in my house, I knew it was
futile. She was gone.

I looked down at Mark accusingly.

"You let her leave you?" I asked.

Mark showed me his teeth, and I growled.

"Fuck!" I yelled,

Then a thought occurred to me.

Although I'd sent her a text message to ride with Griffin to my
place, maybe she missed the memo.

Maybe they were still there.

Maybe.

The drive to the office was one of blinding worry, and it only
multiplied when I got to the office and found it empty as well.

"Fuck!" I yelled.

"She's gone," Alison said from behind me.

I whirled around and stared at her.

"What?" I asked, the calm in my voice deceptive.

I was about as far from calm as I could get.

"Gone."

"What?" I asked, my belly tightening into a painful knot.

"I'm sorry," Alison said. "But it had to be done."

"What do you mean it had to be done?" I barked. "She has a fucking man out there trying his best to make my life, and hers, a living hell. And after what happened today, I wouldn't put it past Agent Fry to start stooping to lower levels. Such as `killing her` lower levels. She can't survive out there on her own!"

Alison's head turned.

"You bought her a dog; a dog that she left here, even though she loved him with all her heart," Alison started.

My mouth dropped open.

"How'd she find that out?" Was my mouth on the floor? Because it sure as hell felt like it was at learning that she found out about the protection dog I bought her. I'd planned that out perfectly! She shouldn't have known anything at all about the dog.

"You had her work for you," Alison said, reading my surprise.

I nodded, still not comprehending where exactly she was going with this.

"You had her file in your files," she said with more emphasis.

I shook my head.

"Just tell him, Dove," Peek said walking up behind Alison. His Irish lilt was back in his voice, full force. "It's not like you to let him squirm like this."

Alison smiled at her husband and then turned back to me.

"The file you had on her, Wolf," Alison finally said. "You made a file on her and then left it on your desk for her to file. Which, might I add, is pretty stupid of you if you wanted her to stay."

My brows furrowed. "What are you talking about?"

"Awwww, fuck," Griffin said, sounding downright contrite. "That was me."

"What was you?" I asked, turning slightly so I could keep him and Alison in my sight.

"That was me who put the file there. However, in my defense, I didn't know what was in the file. I just put it there along with about ten other files that came from the interoffice mail," Griffin replied. "Got a shipment in last Tuesday, and I was in a hurry and put them on your desk instead of mine because yours was closer. That was the day Lenore had some perv in her store jacking off in the middle of the aisle."

I closed my eyes and thought back to that night, remembering it vividly because I'd had to come back into town with Nathan and taken Griffin to the hospital because he needed a tetanus shot and a few stitches since the creep had bit him before Griffin had taken him down with a right hook to his face.

"Why'd we get a file in on Raven?" I asked, starting to pace our small office.

"I can answer that," a deep voice that I didn't recognize said from the door that led to Mig's part of the office.

My head snapped around and a gun was suddenly in my hand, pointing at the chest of the stranger who I'd seen standing at Agent Josh Fry's side earlier in the day.

A man I'd just gotten a dossier on from Travis.

"What the fuck?" Griffin barked.

I chanced a glance over at him to see that he too had his firearm out and pointed at the newcomer.

The newcomer, however, wasn't fazed by having five guns pointed at him.

Hell, even Alison had hers out.

"I had the file sent over to you, but I had no clue that it was going to work against my favor, rather than with it," the man said dryly. "I was hoping to give you her information and entice you back to her, not cause her to run away from you."

My brows rose.

"What do you happen to know about all of this, Raphael?" I asked, showing him a little bit of my hand, letting him know I wasn't completely clueless.

Raphael's grin flashed before he walked further into the room.

"I have a vested interest in the well-being of my sister." Raphael took a seat at my desk and waited.

It didn't take long.

Alison and I both exploded at once.

But it was Griffin's outburst that surprised me the most.

"What the fuck do you mean, sister?" Griffin asked. "From what I've seen, Raven was alone. She didn't have one single person at her back other than this fucking club. So, where have you been, motherfucker?"

My sentiments exactly.

"I'm too far undercover – and have been since I found out about her – that I could only do so much. Basically, just watch and try to take care of her from afar," Raphael said, sounding strained and a little bit sad.

I shook my head.

"Well, right now I'm worried about finding Raven before she gets hurt," I said, my hands fisting.

"She's fine," Alison and Raphael said at the same time.

My brows rose.

"How?" I asked.

"I have Core on her," Alison said at the same time that Raphael said, "I have a man on her."

"And what exactly is your role in all this?" I asked, stopping at the corner of the room to lean one shoulder on the wall.

My stance said 'calm' but I was feeling anything but. I was feeling all kinds of things right then.

Anger that Raven left. Disappointment that she didn't talk to me before she left.

I thought I'd shared my feelings with her. I thought she understood the connection.

Now I come to find out that the connection we were feeling wasn't as tight as I thought it was.

The final emotion I was feeling was fear.

Fear that this whole thing was going to blow up in my face. Fear that something would happen to Raven. Fear that my son would lose a father for the second time in his tiny life.

"My role is to investigate Agent Fry," Raphael said immediately. "I learned that he seems to have a little unhealthy obsession with my sister, and I don't really like it."

"So you wormed yourself into this investigation?" Griffin challenged him.

Peek snorted.

"Precisely."

I sighed.

"How about you tell us what the fuck is going on, and why Agent Fry has a hard on for us, and we'll figure something out from there," I offered through clenched teeth, already fucking tired of all of the bullshit.

Raphael leaned his shoulder against the door and scrubbed a hand down his face.

"I started this internal investigation into Fry about eight months ago when there were only hunches on my bosses' parts that there was something more going on than what was on the surface," he explained. "Eight fucking months later, and I'm still stuck in this hellhole trying to drag myself out. Every time I get close to getting out and nailing the bastard, he miraculously shrugs off all possible charges or evidence is lost, and I'm pulled back in. Of course, learning that they had my sister didn't help; there was no way I was getting out while she was still in. Found out they had her in the first place by accident. They didn't know that I was undercover or her brother, but they knew I didn't like that whole kidnapping situation and what was going on with July and Raven. To put the cherry on the cake, they had her under Jensen mother fucking Gordon's thumb. Pretty much forcing my hand and making me work alone on trying to free them both."

"I found out what he was doing to her and was only hours from getting her out myself. Y'all found her faster than I could," he paused. "Been watching you ever since. Took leave from my job when they told me that the budget for this investigation had been depleted and wasn't being replenished, to drop the investigation."

"So now what?" I asked. "You're a vigilante?"

"You could say that," he said. "I'm on medical leave for a gunshot injury that's being persnickety." He grinned devilishly. "I have a feeling it's about to heal up nicely within the next couple of weeks. I'll be back on the job within the next month."

"Goddammit," I growled. "This is so fucked up. I'm still not sure what the fuck I did to warrant him going out of his way to fuck with me."

"He goes to a lot of trouble to make sure the guys he has working for him won't leave. Blackmail, finding exactly what it takes to keep them where he wants to be, and he's got them for good until he no longer needs them," he grinned. "And you single-handedly took down two out of three of them and with them went the entire Southern half of his merchandise acquisition operation.

I crossed my arms.

"That was his own fucking fault."

Raphael grinned, but that grin quickly disappeared moments later.

"He was just playing with you," he said. "He's been too busy trying to get his operation back up and running. You were a toy for him to play with, but one he definitely planned on taking care of at some point. However, after what you did to him today, as well as what you did to the man we found in the river—luckily alive—it means he'll be pulling you off the back burner."

He stood up and stared at me, giving me the full effect of his eyes.

"And I'm here to make sure you have every fucking tool in my arsenal to make sure this fucker pays." His eyes went to the dog at my feet. "Why isn't Marky Mark with my sister?"

I raised an eyebrow at him.

"You."

"Me?"

I nodded in confirmation. "You."

He sighed.

"He's fully trained," Raphael said. "Trained him myself."

I nodded again. "I figured that. He's fucking phenomenal."

Raphael grinned. "I know that."

"Wait," Alison asked. "There are so many misunderstandings here. Raven told me you kept giving the dog looks as if you knew the dog's potential."

"I did know his potential," I said. "It's not hard to understand what he does when I walk into the room and see him clock me the moment I step foot inside. He moves with her, too. She moves left, he moves left with her, positioning himself so that he's between her and any potential harm."

Alison's eyes widened.

"That's so cool," she looked down at the dog. "He looks so normal."

Raphael snorted and whistled.

The dog looked up at him but didn't move from my feet.

Although Raphael raised him and trained him, he wasn't his dog anymore. He was Raven's. Raven had his loyalty and his heart, and by extension through her, so did I. He had more of a connection to me than he did to Raphael anymore.

I grinned and gave a raised eyebrow to the surprised look on Raphael's face.

"I like that," he said, knowing instantly what was going on.

"I do too," I agreed.

"So, where is she?" Griffin asked. "My wife is asking for cheesecake. Fucking pregnancy hormones are practically ripping my money from my wallet as fast as it gets there."

"You need to give her time to straighten her head out. She'll come back when she cools down," Raphael offered his two cents. "I know exactly where she is. She's safe."

"Uhh, I hate to say this, but I don't agree with him," Alison said. "I agreed that she needed to leave, but I didn't agree that you shouldn't follow. She deserves to be chased. She needs someone to go after her, no matter how many times she leaves. She's never had someone do that for her before."

Pain flashed across Raphael's face—there and gone within a few milliseconds.

I decided to ignore him.

I had things to do, and he wasn't one of them.

Heading to my desk, I pocketed my phone, keys, and wallet.

"Griffin, will you get one of the boys to watch over my kid while I'm gone? And someone watch Mark?" I asked. "I should be back by midafternoon tomorrow."

Griffin nodded, saluting me half-assed before picking up his phone and making a call, I assumed to the cops that were in the district where Nathan was with his grandmother.

I started across the room but stopped.

Before I left to find my wayward woman, I needed to address something first, which was why I stopped in front of Peek.

"We're going to have a talk about this," I hissed.

Peek nodded in understanding.

"It was me…" Peek held his hand up and stopped Alison's apology.

"You came between one of our members and his woman, Alison. I know you meant well, but this isn't the time to defend yourself," Peek said, his Irish brogue thick and brooking no room for argument.

Alison's lips tightened. "Fine."

With that, I left, heading straight to my bike, stopping only for a few minutes to give Core a call to make sure I knew where she was headed.

I was right. The woman was too sentimental.

CHAPTER 17

Tis the season for warmer weather. Please be sure to dress for the body you have, not for the body you want.
- Public service announcement to men and women everywhere.

Raven

I felt the covers slide down to my ass, and my eyes flew open.

Before I could move a muscle, though, I was pinned down with a hard body on top of me.

Before I could struggle, my hands were pinned up above my head, and my mouth was covered with a large hand.

The way the room was situated in the parking lot, added on to the fact that I closed the blackout curtains before I'd gone to bed, meant I couldn't see a damn thing.

I could smell, though.

I could feel.

And I knew, without a shadow of a doubt, that the man on my back was Wolf.

He didn't say a word as I felt him move against me.

His hard cock was pressed against the seam of my legs, hard and insistent.

I started to thrash so I could get away from him, but he only tightened everything.

His thighs that were holding mine captive. His hand that was keeping the words from spewing from my mouth. His other hand that was holding mine in an unyielding grip above my head.

I couldn't move a damn thing except for the lower half of my legs, and they were doing no good because the only thing that could reach him was the tips of my toes, and that was only hurting me and not him when I connected with his flesh.

"Go ahead and struggle," he growled against the back of my neck. "I'm so fucking tired of your bullshit."

I struggled harder, hating the anger that was in his voice, all of it directed at me.

That wasn't the way it was supposed to go! I was supposed to be mad at him!

He was the asshole that chose to play dumb instead of just telling me the truth.

"Get off!" I screamed into his hands, bucking my hips.

He chuckled against my neck, then his tongue darted out and licked the line at the base of my neck that he could reach without actually moving his body.

I started to shiver.

In anger and arousal.

The two emotions were powerful by themselves, but together…well, let me just tell you…it was fucking explosive!

The moment Wolf parted my legs with his knees, so fucking rough and intent on what he was doing, my body went electric.

He pressed the head of his hot and hard cock up against my opening, and I melted.

I should've fought.

Should've screamed and hoped the neighbors heard me.

But I didn't.

I pushed my hips up, and he grunted with approval.

His hand came off my mouth, and latched onto my hip.

His other hand still held both of mine in place, though, giving me that sense of being taken.

And he did take me.

Hard. Rough. Fast.

"Fuck!" I yelled, my pussy throbbing around his thick cock.

He didn't slow in his ministrations. He took me so roughly that it was nearly brutal, and I couldn't stop the cries coming from me.

He read the situation, though, and his hand left my hip to circle around the front.

His skillful fingers went to my clit, so sensitive and distended, causing me to close my eyes in relief.

He didn't slow his thrusts. Didn't try to hide his strength from me.

His balls slapped against my clit with every push of his hips.

Our skin was slapping together, the sound filling the hotel room, only adding to the erotic show that was already happening between my legs.

He grunted and suddenly let go of my hands, sitting up straight so he could get the angle he wanted.

"Lift your leg up," he pushed the back of one thigh, and I lifted it, hoping that was what he wanted.

"Plant your foot on the bed up by your hand," he instructed me, moving my foot for me.

The move had him going even deeper, and a low groan escaped my lips.

"Oh, fuck," I gasped. "Oh, my God."

He chuckled and shoved forward, stretching not just the limits of my flexibility, but the limits of my pussy.

He filled me so deeply that I could feel the coarseness of his pubic hairs rubbing deliciously against my backside.

"God."

My vocabulary was severely lacking, but I couldn't find the ability to speak clearly with the way he was filling me up.

The way his hard chest was pressed against my back.

The way his large hands held me so tightly, almost as if he never wanted to let me go.

Then he started to come.

The feel of his hot come filling me up so fully had elation coursing through my body.

The orgasm that was building waned, but I didn't worry that he'd leave me hanging.

The moment every last drop was out of his cock and pooling inside of me, he pulled out and rolled me to my back, his still hard cock coming down to grind into my pussy.

"Yes," he breathed. "That's it."

With it being so dark, the only thing I could do was close my eyes and visualize what he looked like above me.

His hair was likely falling into his eyes, and his beard was likely unkempt at this early an hour.

His muscles were probably straining the confines of his skin as he held himself aloft over the length of my body.

And his dick was probably red and angry just like his attitude.

"Fucking come," he ordered, his mouth slamming down on mine.

I wrapped my arms around his shoulders, pushing my nipples into the coarse hair dusted in a light spattering over his chest.

I refused to come, though.

Not yet.

Not without him going with me.

"I'll make you come," he said, sliding his hard cock back inside of me.

I closed my eyes as my body arched off the bed.

He laughed against my mouth.

My pussy clenched.

And the next twenty minutes were a lesson in humility—for me and not him.

His strength was mind-boggling. He didn't come unless he wanted to. He also refused to let me come unless he wanted me to.

Even when I'd given up and tried to.

The moment he sensed me close, he'd pull out, or stop, or change his rhythm.

By the time he was ready to come again, I was a big puddle of goo.

Begging and crying for release.

Begging for him to give me what I needed.

"Please," I cried, real tears starting to course down my cheeks.

"Fuck me," he growled, pumping into me hard and fast.

He gave me what I'd been searching for, pinching my clit with his finger and his thumb, finally allowing me to implode.

Wolf followed directly behind me, grunting as his abs flexed.

I gasped and pulled away from him, my anger returning in full force.

Wolf's come hit my thigh, and he growled and pulled me back roughly before slamming back inside of me, holding me still after he finished inside of me entirely.

"Pig," I mumbled into the pillows.

"Shithead," he mumbled, pulling back.

His cock left me in a wet rush, and I rolled and sat up in bed, uncaring that I was leaking everywhere.

"What are you doing here?" I yelled at him, staring in the direction I thought he was sitting.

The light turned on behind me, and I felt heat rush to my head as I realized he was nowhere near where I thought he was.

His eyes held amusement as I adjusted to the new light.

"What are you doing here?" I repeated myself, anger making my voice wobble.

The anger fell flat on Wolf, his eyes too focused on my breasts. Obviously, my voice wasn't the only thing wobbling.

I hastily grabbed the pillow that I'd recently been screaming into and slapped it across the front of my naked body.

"And why am I naked?" I all but yelled.

Wolf's amused eyes came up to mine.

"You looked hot?" he tried.

I bared my teeth at him and made my way to my knees, the wetness between my legs making me uncomfortable.

Growling under my breath, I used the pillow to try to shield my body, but being the curvy woman I was, it didn't hide much—if anything—at all.

I used it anyway, though, and walked straight to the bathroom and slammed the door.

Wolf caught it before I could lock it, though, and I chose to give him that boon, instead focusing on turning the shower on scalding hot and stepping inside.

The shriek that passed through my lips didn't do anything to control my anger, either.

I hated showing weakness when I was mad.

Which in turn caused me to start crying.

Sobs tore out of my throat, partially because of the anger I felt, but also because of the relief that was pouring through my body.

He'd come for me.

I'd, literally, only been in the hotel for three hours, meaning he came to look for me way before I hoped he would.

"You're crying," he said smartly.

A laugh burst free of my lungs.

"Yeah," I sniffled, leaning my head back until I could douse my hair. "I'm crying."

"The file. It's not mine. Griffin had it done. And I have a lot of things to tell you. But whatever's going on in your head, whatever you misconstrued to be true, isn't. You should've talked to me before you left again."

I pursed my lips and turned.

"You're telling me you didn't buy Marky Mark for me?" I asked. "I priced those dogs! Those run upwards to tens of thousands of dollars. If you bought him for me, I'm paying you back!"

"If you're paying me back, why'd you leave him?" he asked.

"I left him because I wasn't thinking straight," I admitted.

It was true. I'd regretted leaving him almost from the moment I left. I contemplated turning around multiple times during my trip, and had nearly done it about half of those times.

The only thing that truly stopped me from making that U turn, though, was losing the will to leave again.

I was so upset, so freakin' hurt that I needed time to think. I couldn't think surrounded by Wolf. The man was overwhelming.

Like earlier. Had I been in the right frame of mind when he woke me up, I would've resisted him.

I would've told him no.

I wouldn't have melted for his body.

Then I laughed humorlessly.

I would never stand a chance against the power of Wolf.

And not his strength.

The sheer force of will that surrounded the man was outstanding. He was like the sun, pulling everything into his gravitational field without even trying.

"You're lying," I said tiredly as I reached for the bottle of complimentary shampoo the hotel so conveniently left in the shower.

"I don't lie," Wolf stated matter of factly. "I tell it how it is. I don't sugar coat things, even for you. Like telling you that you were stupid to leave. You had no money. You had no protection. You had no clue how far this man that's fucking with our lives is willing to go, and that's even after you saw that some man tried to beat the shit out of me with my son in my arms not even two nights ago."

So, he was angry.

Really, really angry.

That I could tell right off the bat.

He hid it so well, though, that sometimes it was hard to tell until Wolf's anger was staring you straight in the face.

And let me tell you something, an angry Wolf was a scary Wolf.

His eyes seemed to glow as they stared at me.

He clearly wasn't happy with me.

Well that made two of us, because I was none too pleased with him as well.

"You and me are from the same town," I said. "There's no way in hell that you don't know about me, something that didn't occur to me until I was leaving this afternoon. I was the town slut. There's no way in hell you *didn't* hear about me."

His eyes darkened. "Don't call yourself that."

"Well, if the shoe fits!" I screamed at him.

He took a step forward, and kept coming until my back was pinned against the cold tiled wall.

"I said don't. Talk. Like. That," he said through gritted teeth. "We do what we have to do to survive. You did what you needed to do to get you through your shit existence." He stopped. "You obviously know nothing about me if you think that I'd think that about you. You forget that I know you. I know for a fact that you're no slut. Because if you were a slut, I'd be a goddamn angel that didn't have black marks times infinity on my soul."

I wasn't really a slut.

Everyone just called me that. Treated me like that.

Sleep with one football player under the bleachers, and suddenly every football player thinks he can get him some.

It wasn't true.

I'd only ever had four sexual partners in my life.

One in high school. One in college, and Jensen.

Then there was Wolf.

Although none of the others held a candle to Wolf.

He was in a league of his own, not only in the bedroom department, but in life in general.

Wolf was everything I ever wanted, and the one thing I didn't think I deserved.

"That's the problem, Wolf," I said tiredly. "I don't know anything about you. I know that you lost your wife and child in utero. I know that you have a sister. I know that you work as a Texas Ranger. But that's it. I literally know nothing else about you."

His eyes darkened.

"What?" I asked. "You're annoying me."

His mouth tipped up into a grin.

Then he lifted his hand to bring it up to his hair. Then he shifted his hand so my fingers slid through his hair.

"Feel that?" he rasped.

Trying to force myself from delighting in the feel of his hair, I started to sift my fingers around and froze when I felt the undeniable feel of a raised scar that had to be at least six inches in length.

"Is that…" I started.

He nodded his head and I swallowed thickly.

Then he picked my other hand up, and shifted it to the back of his head, and my stomach started to roll.

"Where did it enter?" I asked, knowing before he even said where it entered.

"The back of my head," he said. "Entered just under the little knot at the bottom of my skull and came out above my left ear."

His eyes went far away as he started to talk.

"I remember turning around, doing what the guy asked, and then…nothing." He looked down into my eyes once again. "Woke up in a hospital room two days later, unable to talk and could barely lift my hand up two inches off the bed."

I nodded my head, remembering that part.

His wife had been shot after him, and they'd laid bleeding together, bleeding out.

The cops had been called due to a noise disturbance when the shots were fired; the cops had arrived only to find something much worse than they could imagine.

"The man that shot everyone…" I said, hesitating. "I'm glad he's dead."

Wolf finally smiled, and the smile was anything but pretty.

"You and me both, Sweetheart," he replied, dropping his forehead to mine.

"I am a bad person," he started. "But you make me want to be a better person."

My fingers in his hair slipped free, and I wrapped them around his tight shoulders.

"You look like something else is on your mind," I guessed.

Wolf sighed and moved away from me, letting my body go as he reached for the soap.

The tiny sliver of soap that the hotel provided looked infinitesimal in his large, deeply tanned hand.

He closed his hand around it and ran it under the water before bringing it to his body to rub roughly.

My eyes watched him move, and although I'd just found release with him only moments before, my body started to throb with new feelings.

That was what that man did to me, though; made me feel.

Made me feel when I didn't want to feel.

"I don't know how to tell you something, and I'm wondering if at this juncture in time if it would be a good thing or a bad thing," he hesitated.

I smiled at him.

"Does it have to do with why I left?" I asked curiously.

He shook his head.

"I didn't buy Marky Mark for you," he said carefully.

"Then who did?" I questioned.

"Your brother."

CHAPTER 18

It's not parenting until you've ruined your child's life simply by serving them dinner.
-Fact of Life

Wolf

"Where'd you leave your baseball shoes?" Raven yelled loudly into the phone.

I pulled the phone away from my ear, checked the connection, and placed it back against my ear.

"The last time I saw his cleats they were in a box beside his bed," I pursed my lips. "Try the toy box. I saw him move everything into it the other day when he cleaned."

A sigh of frustration filled the line, and I had to hide my smile.

"Why is Casten here and not you?" she asked me as she rushed around the house.

I could only guess what she was doing, but I did have experience trying to find Nathan's shit. We had two shirts, two pairs of socks, and two pairs of pants for this very reason.

What we did not have two of were his shoes, his bat, or his glove.

Which happened to be the only things he lost.

"I gotta go or this kid of yours isn't going to make it to the game on time," she murmured. "Are you on your way?"

I looked at the empty booth in front of me.

"No," I said. "I'll likely be late."

She sighed.

"Casten's taking me to the game, then?" she asked.

"No," I said. "He's not."

There was a momentary pause, then a hesitant question that made my heart stutter. "Who's taking me, then?"

It'd been a week and a half since I'd picked her up at the Texas/Oklahoma border.

Eight days since I'd told her about her brother, and not a single one of those had she said a word about him.

In fact, she studiously ignored anything and everything that had to do with Raphael.

Which, at this juncture in time, wasn't such a bad thing since Raphael had so much shit on his plate.

That shouldn't have stopped him from at least making contact.

He didn't, though, and Raven had refused to say a single word about the man.

I knew for a fact that the two of them knew each other well enough to have an inkling at who the other was.

But, in all my time with Raven, I hadn't once heard about Raphael, and Raphael refused to share just why exactly she refused to talk about anything that had to do with her brother.

A brother that was, in fact, her brother.

I had the DNA test done to prove it.

For not only my peace of mind, but Raven's as well, should she choose to question anything.

Yet she hadn't.

And that was why Raphael was coming over tonight.

He didn't know that Raven was going to be there. All he knew was that Raven was going out with a few friends with a couple of men to watch her.

And I guess, technically, she was.

She was going to a wedding shower with Ridley's soon to be wife, Freya.

All of the men's wives would be there. Lenore, Annie, Tasha, Kitt and Alison.

And all of the kids would be watched by the men—all the men but two, who would be watching the ladies like a hawk.

Although, Raphael was supposed to be late coming in. He had some news he was going to share with us (us being the Uncertain Saints, not Raven) and wouldn't be there until after his normal work day ended.

Apparently, Agent Fry kept them all busy doing bogus work to make his paperwork nice and pretty when, in reality, all they were doing was just enough work on the computer to make things nice and air tight—while after hours they were busy doing their illegal side business.

"Core's taking you," I said. "And he's bringing you back, so make sure you stick tight to him tonight. Don't leave with anyone else, okay?"

Raven let out a relieved breath, and then started moving through the room again.

"I found it!" Nathan shrieked, causing a smile to burst out over my face.

"Fuck me!" Goody, my informant who was currently making me late, gasped as he yanked the door to my office open and started around the corner of the filing cabinets. "I'm about to die!"

"I gotta go, baby," I said, well used to the tactics that Goody used to gain attention. "I'll be a little late for his game, but hopefully not much."

"Okay," she hesitated. "I love you."

Joy surged through me, and I started to say something more when Goody started to reach for me.

"I love you too, baby girl."

I hung up and shoved my phone into my pocket, glaring at the man that'd practically crawled over the top of my desk to get to my hand.

"What the fuck do you want?" I asked. "Get off me and stop touching me with those disgusting fingers."

Goody bared his teeth, and I had to stifle the urge to grimace.

Goody had disgusting teeth.

I doubted he'd seen the inside of a dentist's office in ten years, if not more.

"You have to help me," he said. "Why weren't you at our usual meeting spot?"

I growled in frustration.

"Because you decided to fuck me over and be late yourself," I said. "And it's not that much of a difference. You walked through my backdoor instead of meeting me at the backdoor. There's little difference in those two distances."

Goody's face started to twitch, and I wondered when his last hit was.

I'd met him when he was trying to get clean off of meth, and had tried to get him on the straight and narrow by offering him some money to become an informant.

Turns out, he liked the money, and still informed, but he had no qualms about spending the money he got informing on his next fix.

"What's that look on your face for?" he asked. "And did you see that man with the creepy eyes?"

I looked at him, then looked out the front window which wasn't nearly as visible now with the filing cabinets moved from that space.

"What guy with the creepy eyes?" I asked him.

"He followed me," he said.

"Followed you from where?" I persisted.

"From the river." He rolled his eyes heavenward. "Why are you being so dense?"

I refrained from beating him upside the head, but only because I knew if I touched his hair I wasn't sure what would come out of it.

I suspected he had lice, and that would be one of the better things I might find in that mat of stuff he called hair.

"Goody," I started. "How about you stay on topic here."

"Fine," he said. "I was at the diner parking lot where I was meeting a deal…umm, friend. And we were around the back of the diner next to where the dumpsters used to be when I heard a boat pull into the dock in front of us."

The diner he was talking about was completely surrounded by water. The people that owned it hadn't been able to get to it except by boat for over two weeks now, and it wasn't looking good any time in the future, either, seeing as we were supposed to be hit with another six inches this weekend.

The diner used to be a pretty popular spot to meet and greet friends when it was open, but now that it was closed, it wasn't useful.

The road leading to the diner wasn't open either, for about a mile in fact.

"And?" I asked, eager to hurry this along.

"And I was curious, so I got a little bit closer and listened to what they were saying," he continued.

I wanted to pull my hair out.

"And what were they saying, Goody?" I asked patiently.

"They were talking about some deal and shipment that was supposed to come through in the next couple of days. The only one there was the crazy eyed man and a Hispanic man I couldn't see," he explained.

"Then how do you know he's Hispanic?"

"Because I could hear his accent, dude. He was clearly talking in Spanish," Goody rolled his eyes.

I snorted.

"And they were talking about meeting there in two nights, trading something for something, and then parting ways," Goody grinned, and my stomach did that churning shit again. "I got his license plate number."

"His license plate number."

I waited for him to change his story, but he stuck with it.

"Yes!"

"On a boat?" I asked with incredulity. "Goody, boats don't have fuckin' license plates!"

"Yes," he said. "He had it in his wallet."

I wanted to strangle him.

I'd seriously be doing the world a favor by doing it, too.

"License," I explained to him, even if it was futile. "You saw his license."

"Yes!" he cried. "And he followed me here."

"How do you know he followed you here?" I questioned, standing up and stuffing my phone into my pocket.

"Because he pulled his boat out at the same time I did, and then drove in this direction," he responded, his voice laced with impatience that I wasn't understanding his words.

"Gotcha," I nodded. "What did his license say?"

"It said that he was an FBI."

***

I pulled my bike up next to Core's truck and threw the kickstand down.

A loud roar from the field that Nathan was playing on raised through the night, and I swung my leg up and off my bike.

My feet squished in the wet mud, and I dropped the helmet onto the seat before taking off across the parking lot.

"Yo!" I yelled the moment I was close enough. "Core, what's the score?"

Core, aka Apple, looked up and smiled.

"Winning three to nothing," he called, returning his eyes to the game.

I noticed that he didn't face the game completely, though, and he'd parked his charge along with his wife at the bleachers directly beside him.

Raven looked up when she heard me call out, and a smile brightened her face.

"You made it!" she cried. "Come sit down, Nathan's on deck."

I finished my jog to her side, and then bent over to drop a kiss on her lips.

"Awwww," I heard a familiar voice say. "That's too cute!"

I looked up and grinned at Hannah.

"Shut your face," I said. "We playing Reggie?"

Hannah nodded and pointed. "She's the catcher right now."

I followed her pointing and a smile broke out over my face.

"That's the cutest thing I've ever seen," I admitted. "Love the curls in the back, too."

Hannah grinned. "She wanted to play baseball, and you were the one to tell me that girls were allowed in this league."

I nodded. I sure had said that, and I liked that Hannah listened to what I had to say.

Taking my seat on the right of Raven so I could still speak to Hannah, I turned forward and watched as the little boy at bat swung at the coach's pitch and connected with the ball.

It went about six inches past his feet, and stopped.

"Run!" I yelled at the kid.

The kid, startled by my outburst, looked at me, and I pointed at first base.

"Run, boy!"

The boy jumped and then started running, his fat little legs carrying him as fast as he could possibly move his bulk to first base.

The coach at first base was smiling huge and holding his hand out for a high five.

However, the little kid kept running, and the coach was left hanging.

"Oh, shit," I said. "Run!"

Reggie had the ball, and she was barreling after the kid like the hounds of hell were at her feet, snapping and snarling along to keep pushing her forward.

"Get 'em, baby!" Hannah yelled. "Tag him!"

The entire team was now on their feet, screaming and yelling, jumping and pointing.

"Run, Bagger!" the kids were yelling. "Get home!"

The coach on second base held his hands up as the kid arrived on second, but instead of stopping, he continued to run.

"Mother of God," I breathed. "Jesus Christ, she's gonna get him."

The kid was slow, and it was terrible of me to say, but he was overweight and didn't run all that fast.

The kid had heart, though, I'd give him that.

Reggie tossed the ball expertly to the kid on third, but the kid was too busy bending down to pick dandelions to catch the ball.

Bagger, which must've been the kid's name since I could now hear his mother yelling it at my side, rounded third.

The dandelion kid finally realized that the ball was at his feet, and blew the dandelion as he picked the ball up and chucked it in the direction of Reggie, who was now once again on home.

"Jesus," Hannah said. "Move out of the way, baby. He's not going to stop."

Reggie moved over just in time for the kid to tumble into home, rolling on his side all the way across the plate.

"Oh, sweet baby Jesus," the mother of the kid sat down next to my feet. "That kid is going to be the death of me."

I laughed and patted her back.

"He did good, Ma'am," I said to her, my eyes going back to the game as I watched Reggie put her hands on her hips and glare at the little kid that was barely up to his feet.

"Thank you," the mom said, a wide smile on her face.

"Good job, Buddy," the coach said, drawing my attention.

I nodded my head at the guy and looked down to see Raven rest her head against my knee.

"He did good," Raven said. "That kid was like a freight train, though."

I snorted and dropped my hand to her head.

"The best players are," I agreed. "Alright, Nathan! Get 'er done, boy!"

Nathan nodded his head, something that hit me straight in the heart.

Seeing him doing that was nearly breathtaking as I recalled a vision of his father doing much the same thing.

Nathan took a couple of practice swings.

"Swing for the fence, Nate!" Raven yelled.

I didn't have any doubt in my mind that the kid would—he was his father's son, after all.

My head tilted back as I let my eyes drift up to the painted white sign on the fence.

There were names of each and every kid that ever hit a homerun, and on the very top was Nathan's biological father, Darren Cox.

"What are you looking at?" Raven asked curiously.

I pointed up.

"That's Darren, Nathan's dad," I told her. "He was the first kid to hit an out-of-the park, over-the-fence home run."

"Seriously?" she asked. "That's pretty awesome."

It was. I'd worked my ass off endlessly to try to get my name up there, and never accomplished it, not even when I was older.

Darren, though, had his name on each and every field from little league all the way up to his high school baseball team.

"Catcher, you ready?" the umpire asked Reggie.

"Yes, Sir," Reggie answered cutely.

Hannah snickered at my back.

"What?" I asked her.

"Your manners are coming out in her," she answered. "Raven, has he gotten on to you yet about eating?"

Raven leaned forward, practically laying across my lap, so she could see Hannah.

"Oh, my God," she whispered as if I couldn't hear her. "He's terrible. Elbows, Raven. Don't you know how to use a fork, Raven? Close your mouth, Raven, nobody wants to see your food."

So, poor table manners were a pet peeve of mine, sue me.

Hannah and Raven took turns trading lines that I apparently said but couldn't remember saying, so I placed my hand on the hem of Raven's shorts and started to slide them upwards.

She instantly stopped what she was doing and sat back down again.

Hannah, none the wiser, pointed.

"Ball!" the umpire yelled.

Nathan looked back at me, and I nodded my head at him before I glared at the coach.

This was becoming an every game occurrence between the coach and my kid.

The coach, Jobert Clay, graduated with me.

He hated my guts, and apparently, that hate not only still burned all these years later, it apparently crossed over generations and translated to my kid.

The coach caught my glare and returned it full force before tossing the ball once more at my kid, narrowly missing his body with the ball.

The ball wasn't one of the soft ones like last year. No, this one was a fucking hard ball, and that mother fucker was throwing it at my kid's body.

I stood up, dislodging my hands from Raven's body, and started down the bleachers until my hands curled around the chain link fence.

Jobert, the stupid fucker, sneered at me before rearing back to throw it, and I knew he was about to hit my kid.

"Back up, Kid," I said to Nathan.

He obeyed immediately and stepped out of the batter box just as the ball sailed by his head.

"You fucker," I said, shaking the chain link fence in front of me. "I'm going to kill you."

With just one look on Jobert's part, I started walking around the fence and turned into the Rocker's dugout.

Once I made it out onto the field, Jobert stood up from his knee and glared.

"You can't be on the field," he informed me haughtily.

I looked over at the umpire. "You have any problem with me pitching to my kid?"

The umpire's face went to the tattoo on my forearm, then raised his arm to show me his Marine Corps. "None at all."

I grinned and held my hand out for the ball that the umpire picked up.

"Excuse me," I shouldered Jobert to the side.

He moved, but just barely and was still crowding me on the mound.

"You'll have to move out of the way, Coach. Can't have two pitchers on the field," the umpire urged Jobert to move with a sweep of his hand.

Jobert, the loser, growled under his breath and jogged to the dugout where he took a seat with a harrumph.

I grinned and turned back to my kid.

"You ready, boy?" I asked him.

He nodded enthusiastically and squared his shoulders before stepping back into the batter's box.

"Ready, Dad."

Pride filled my throat as I tossed the ball to him like I did any other time we practiced.

It wasn't a bitch throw, either.

It was a real one.

Sure, I didn't put as much heat on it as I could have, but it wasn't a pitch any other kid could hit.

Nathan swung and missed, and little Miss Reggie caught the ball like a pro and threw it back.

Uncle Wolf didn't raise no slackers.

Nathan looked at me, grinned as he took his place once again, and then nodded his head.

I threw the next one, and knew instantly that he'd hit it.

What I didn't expect was for my nearly six-year-old son to hit a home fucking run.

It sailed just barely over the back fence, but it went, and it counted.

Mother fucker, but did it count.

CHAPTER 19

*There's nothing like taking your bra off when you walk in your
door after a long hard day of having boobs.
-Raven's secret thoughts*

Raven

"I had a really great time with you ladies," I said to the room full
of women.

Lenore waved her hand as if to clear away my words.

"We enjoyed getting to spend some time with you again," Lenore
replied as she leaned forward. "But we all have a burning question
to ask you."

I blinked, then tilted my head slightly. "What?"

"Does Wolf really have as naughty a personality as he comes off as
having?" Annie asked. "He's always so dark and standoffish. Like
Mig used to be, but way worse."

I smiled at her.

"Wolf isn't dark. He just doesn't talk unless he wants to," I
explained. "Engage him in a conversation, and see what comes of
it. Trust me, you won't be disappointed."

"I don't think Wolf could disappoint anyone," Tasha put in. "He
gave me a ride once. I felt like I was cheating on my man just by
having my arms around him."

I laughed then.

Yeah, Wolf was beautiful. He was also taken. Very, *very* taken.

And a tingle of jealousy rolled up my spine at hearing all the stories that were floating around that surrounded my man and his good intentions.

"Do you need any help taking these to the car?" I asked Freya.

Freya shook her head. "No. I have a man for that. Although, I haven't seen him in a while."

"That's because the men are having a powwow on the porch with someone."

I blinked, surprised by that.

"I thought that they were meeting at the clubhouse," I said. "That's what I heard Wolf say to whomever he was speaking to on the phone earlier when they called."

"Something happened," Annie said as she licked the rest of the salt off her margarita glass. "I saw them with their heads pressed together. Then some man showed up."

A burning feeling started to tickle my belly.

"What'd the man look like?" I asked, standing up.

"Tall, dark. Bright white smile and brown eyes. Brown hair. Black clothes. Couldn't tell much more than that because they disappeared around the side of the house when they saw me snooping," Tasha grinned unrepentantly.

"You should've been more covert about it," Kitt, Core's wife, said. "How do you think I know the things I do?"

"Because you fuck the answers out of your man, that's how," Tasha said. "My man, however, knows the importance of keeping his trap shut."

Kitt snorted. "You're full of shit. Just last week you told me that you heard Wolf enjoyed spanking and tying people up from Core. I know for a fact that Wolf didn't just offer that information up to anyone and everyone that wanted to know."

I gritted my teeth at the irrational surge of jealousy that rocketed through me at knowing that these women knew about Wolf's kinks.

"I also heard that Core told you about Lenore being pregnant," Kitt said.

I sighed and stood up.

"Be right back. Have to pee," I told them and darted out of the door of Freya and Ridley's living room.

I stopped at the bathroom and did my business before sneaking out of the bathroom so they wouldn't hear me go. Then hurried to the backdoor and slipped outside.

I peered around the corner, and I could tell instantly that my attempt to be quiet had not gone unseen.

Mainly because the moment I poked my head around, Wolf's big ass body was just there, stopping me.

"What are you doing?" he asked.

"I'm trying to see who you're hiding out here," I said. "What are you doing here anyway? I thought y'all were going to the clubhouse."

"We were, but then something came up," he said.

"What came up?" I asked.

"The water, which somehow managed to untie our boats that are now nowhere to be found. Hence, why we're here," he explained with a grin on his face.

I pursed my lips.

"Good enough," I said. "But what are you hiding?"

"That would be me," a familiar voice said, whipping my head around to my back so fast that I likely sustained whiplash.

"What are *you* doing here?" I snarled.

"Now, is that any way to talk to your brother?" he teased.

I bared my teeth at him.

"I don't have a brother," I said stubbornly.

Okay, I really did have a brother, but this man wasn't him.

Not anymore, at least.

He lost the right to that title the day he left me to join the military and didn't look back.

True, I'd been ten at the time, but it still left a lasting impression on me.

He'd been my rock, my everything, and he'd left me in that shitty assed foster home without a backwards glance.

I didn't care if he tried to come back years later, which happened to be around the time that Wolf came into my life.

It was too little too late, and I didn't care what kind of good excuses he had. The only thing in my mind that could logically explain his distance from me was death, and by the looks of him, he was most certainly not dead.

"I'm going to go back inside," I said to no one in particular. "Have fun discussing whatever it is you're discussing."

With that, I went back inside, and didn't spare my ex-brother another glance.

***

"Alright," Wolf said the moment he came back into the bedroom we were now sharing at his house. "Tell me what the hell is going on with you and your brother and don't leave a goddamn thing out."

I lifted my lip up in a silent snarl before totally ignoring the statement.

"Did you get Nathan settled back at Nancy's?" I tried to divert his attention.

When I saw his look that clearly said it wasn't going to work, I lifted my shirt up and over my head.

His eyes zeroed in on my breasts, his pupils dilating as his breathing started to increase.

I'd give him credit, though. The man had control.

Wolf turned his back on me and lifted his own shirt, tossing it to the floor at his feet.

I walked around him, picked up his shirt, and then walked both his and mine to the hamper that was about two feet in front of him.

"Nathan's currently asleep in his bed, and Nancy was about to follow him as soon as I left," he said to my back. "What are you doing?"

His question sounded strained, but I didn't chance a look behind me. I didn't want to run out of courage. If I got a good look at his face, at his worry for me and the situation he'd inadvertently placed me in by getting involved in something that was sure to piss off the man, whomever he was, then I'd lose the courage.

Pushing down my panties, I presented him with my naked back; the only thing blocking his view of the split between my ass cheeks was my hair.

My hair was down and curly, a small section of it hanging down to my front while the other part went in any and all directions around my head.

"I don't want to talk about anything right now," I said, turning around and presenting him with my front.

His eyes zeroed in on my belly.

"When," he took a large step forward, "did you get that?"

Then, suddenly, Wolfgang Amsel was on his knees at my feet.

His large, tanned hands spanned my hips, his fingers digging into the flesh above my butt, and he stared, eyes transfixed on the newest addition to my ink.

It'd hurt like the dickens to get, too.

His thumbs swept forward, just barely caressing the clear covering over my tattoo.

"You tattooed my name on your body," he said gruffly. "Holy fucking shit."

I smiled.

"I wasn't originally going to go in there to do that," I told him bluntly. "Originally, it was going to be a phoenix, but when I got there, the words just sort of fell out of my mouth."

"I like it," he said, a surge of possessiveness tinging his words.

I grinned.

"How did you know what it said?" I asked him. "The guy said you couldn't really tell."

He looked up at me like I'd just asked him the stupidest question ever.

"I've been spelling my name for thirty some odd years. I'm pretty sure I can spot when my fuckin' name's been inked into my woman's skin," he muttered.

Then he leaned down and pressed a kiss right above my pubic bone.

His prickly beard mingled with the hairs covering my mound, and I felt a surge of pleasure as I saw how the hairs mingled, becoming one.

"I love you, you know," Wolf admitted. "Fucking loved you for forever."

Something in my belly loosened.

"I left because it was too hard to watch you with another woman," I blurted.

His eyes moved to my face, and I instantly missed the feel of his beard so close to me.

"You what?" he asked in surprise.

"I left," I repeated, "I left because I couldn't stand seeing you with Hannah. Y'all had an instant family, and it was tearing me apart."

He dropped his forehead to my belly.

"I broke up with her that night."

The words hit me like a ton of bricks, and suddenly anger poured through my system.

"You what?" I yelled, my arms going up above my head. "What the hell?"

He sat back on his heels. However, that was only because the push to his shoulders practically forced him away from me. He would've gone further had he not been as quick as he was.

"What?" he asked in confusion. "What'd I say?"

"I make fucking googly eyes at you for months, and nothing. Then I freakin' throw in the towel, and you decide to break up with her?" I was yelling now, full out.

I didn't care, though.

Wolf didn't have any neighbors, and with Nathan at his grandmother's there was nothing and nobody to upset but him with my words.

"What the fuck?" Wolf stood to his feet, both planted apart and ready for whatever came at him. "I didn't think you'd freakin' disappear off the face of the Earth. I gave you my number, and practically told you to call me the moment you got to where you were going. I honestly thought I'd be able to find you faster than I did."

"You didn't find me at all!" I yelled, repeating his earlier words. "Before you brought me back, you flat out told me that you couldn't find me."

He nodded his head.

"That's true," he admitted. "However, that was only by me asking my sister. I was giving you time."

"Time for what?" I crossed my arms over my chest, tired of feeling them flop around every time I moved my hands. "Me to forget you?"

He was on me before I could react.

One second he was standing across the room from me, and the next he was in my space, his face inches from mine.

His beard tickled my chest, and I refused to react, even though everything inside of me urged me to stroke his beard.

Damn his magical bearded powers against my hormones!

"You'll never forget me. I won't let you." He turned me until I was flattened against the bed, his hips pinning mine to the bed, and his strong thighs parting my legs for him to fall in between.

I gasped when I felt his hard body press against me.

Everything, even the inside of his thighs, were hard. His strong, muscular jaw. His tight, forearms that were planted on either side of my head, and his bearded mouth that started to run down the tops of my shoulders.

I weakened even more.

"You wanna know why you'll never forget me?" he rasped, letting the stiff point of his tongue trail along the outer shell of my ear.

"Why?" I pushed my booty up, glad now that I was naked.

Expedience was crucial, especially when I was about to come despite the only contact I had from him was with his hard cock along the length of my ass.

"Because I won't let you. Every time you even seem like you're forgetting me, I'm going to show you, just like I'm about to do, just what you'll be missing by me not being there. I'm going to give you everything I have to give, and then I'm going to pull out more. I'm going to drown you in me, and make it physically impossible for you to ever leave me." He lifted my hips and lined his cock up with my entrance. "You're mine just as I'm yours, and I'll never let you forget that. Not for the next hundred years."

My breath caught in my throat.

"You mean just as much to me, you know," I whispered to him, looking over my shoulder so he could see the sincerity in my eyes. "There's not a day that goes by that I don't fall more in love with you than I was the day before."

He slid the length of his cock through my slit, coating himself in my wetness.

My wetness, I had to point out, was so copious that I was on the verge of being embarrassed.

"That makes two of us," he said. "I didn't think I'd find love like this. I'd resigned myself to a life filled with useless, meaningless hookups for the rest of my life."

"Well, I'm going to be happy to prove to you, for the rest of my life, how much you mean to me." I pushed back. "Now stop teasing me and give me what you're promising, or I'll have to take matters into my own hands."

He growled, and started to press forward, the tip of his cock breaching my entrance, stretching and filling me.

"Condoms," I breathed, pulling forward.

"No condoms." He held my hips steady.

"Yes," I insisted, stiffening slightly. "I'm not on birth control, and you damn well know that's the last thing we need to be worried about right now."

"Our worries should be over by tomorrow night," he said. "So how about you let me worry about what you should be worrying about."

To be honest, that idea sounded heavenly—to have him making the decisions. To have him take all of my worries away, even if only for a few short moments.

So, that's how I ended up letting him slide his cock into my pussy, bare, again. I know we've done this before, but I wasn't thinking straight the last time.

Before Wolf entered my life, anytime someone took me, it was with every single precaution in place. With Wolf, I just knew that he was my one and only and if a baby resulted from this, we would deal.

The sheer freeness of having him inside me bare was so arousing, so very, very wrong, that the moment he finally worked his length fully inside of me, I started to come.

"Oh, God," I breathed, my core muscles clamping tight, and my pussy closing over his cock so hard, that I stopped breathing.

I literally couldn't find it in myself to do that important bodily function.

My vision swam, and my clit sang.

Then his hand came down on my ass once more, and I drew in a sharp breath.

Wolf stayed true to his norm, though, and never said a word.

Instead, he took hold of my hips when I started to collapse, and he pounded inside of me.

Finesse was so far out the window that everything we did was purely out of instinct.

Our breathing came in rough pulls.

My head fell to rest on the mattress, and Wolf's hand automatically went to the falling strands, fisting the back of my hair with such strength that I gasped and threw my head back, inadvertently putting it exactly where he wanted it.

His free hand circled my throat, coming to a rest just above my collarbone to hold me in place.

Then he held me to him as he resumed fucking me.

Using my body as he saw fit.

I surrendered all control over to him.

I was too busy trying to retain the last bit of control that I had, and he was busy losing it.

He felt the moment I gave over to him, and with a deep groan, his movements became rougher and less controlled. Suddenly, the lovemaking turned into something so deep and pure that tears started to fall down my cheeks.

This couldn't be normal, this connection that I had with him. I'd never felt anything like this pure, unaltered passion. This passion we had for each was something that would never, ever fade.

My knees gave out, and instead of falling on top of me like I thought he would do, he pulled me, on my side, curling his big body around me from behind.

He made slow, sweet love to me. Driving in and pulling out, circling his hips almost like we were performing an intimate dance.

And I guess that was what we were doing…only horizontally and in a bed.

With his dick in me.

I was fairly sure most people didn't dance like we did.

That was the only type of dancing Wolf and I would ever be doing, and to be honest, I was A-Okay with that.

Wolf's lips parted, and I felt his soft, hot tongue run along the shell of my ear before he bit it.

My hand went down to my parted thighs, and I let my fingers slip through the folds of my sex, slowly moving down until I found where we were joined.

I let my fingers part in the middle, with Wolf's solid cock thrust between them. The pad of my thumb pressed against my clit, and the orgasm that was building became urgent.

Wolf's head came down to rest against the top of my spine, and I knew he was close.

Which was why I tightened my pelvic muscles and started to stroke my clit.

Wolf groaned before his breath exploded against my neck.

He grunted, his belly tightened, and I felt his cock start to twitch.

Irrationally, I'd hoped that I would feel the splash of his come inside of me, but alas I didn't. And I was so focused on feeling him that I didn't pay attention.

I didn't feel his hand move to my breast.

Didn't feel his thumb move to pinch my nipple until he was already doing it.

My attention to the feeling of him coming was lost with my thoughts, and I gasped as my orgasm rolled over me.

My body bowed, and the only thing that was holding me where I was, was Wolf's grip on my breasts and his cock planted deep.

"Jesus," I breathed, my head falling back limply against his collarbone.

He hummed, letting my breast go and banding his arm tightly just under my breasts.

We lay like that, both of us trying to control our breathing, for long moments.

Then his hand slipped back down to my hip, his fingers caressing the clear plastic that covered my tattoo.

"When the hell did you find time to get a tattoo without me knowing it?" Wolf asked me, still breathless.

"I became friends with the tattoo artist who did my wolf," I explained. "She was able to work me in at lunch. We worked on it solid for an hour before I was back. Core waited outside the room the entire time."

Wolf grinned.

"Did he know what you were doing?" he asked.

I tossed him a look. "No," I said facetiously. "I was at a tattoo artist's place of business and he had no clue what I was doing."

Wolf popped his hand against my ass, and I gasped.

"Wolf!" I growled, trying to dislodge him from my sex and roll over onto my knees. "What the hell?"

He held me steady, keeping himself planted deep, and pulled me in tightly to his chest. His front to my back, his arm up high above my head so my face rested against his bicep.

"Your lip isn't needed, so stow it away when I want your mouth, and you haven't just sucked my soul out of my dick," he said, smoothing the hand that'd just inflicted the damage over my ass to soothe instead of maim this time.

I reached back and pinched him, and he chuckled.

"What?" he asked innocently.

"You know what, dammit," I pinched him again.

He sighed and ran his hand down my backside, up and down, side to side.

The motion was so soothing that I found my eyes becoming heavy even when I didn't want them to be.

Wolf finally slipped free of my sex, and I gasped at the feeling of loss.

"Wolf," I whined.

"You never told me about why you and your brother don't get along," he pushed. "Honey, I need to know. It doesn't take a rocket scientist to figure out that something happened. If he hurt you, I need to know. My instincts are telling me he's solid and that he

236

really wants a relationship with you, but I don't want to continue to put my support at his back if he's hurt you in some way."

I sighed and returned my head back to his shoulder.

"He left me," I whispered into his neck, remembering the pain like it was yesterday. "He was the only constant in life; I relied on him for everything. He kept me sane, protected me against the assholes that were in the foster home with me. Then one day he was just gone, and I was left with no one. My life turned to shit after that, and I blamed him for it. I think I still do, as a matter of fact."

"You don't hate him," Wolf said into my hair. "You're upset, and understandably so. But in your heart, you knew."

"I knew what?" I asked stubbornly.

"Why he left."

I did know.

"They told him he had to go. They said he couldn't take me, and if he tried, they'd send him to jail," I whispered into the darkness. "But I didn't expect him to just completely disappear from my life like that. I expected him to move out, find a job, and stay close by. I never thought he'd just leave me behind and never look back."

"I overheard him saying that he tried to find a job and couldn't. Nobody would hire him because he was the son of someone nobody liked," Wolf replied softly.

"His father wasn't my father. Apparently, his was a loser who scammed about two hundred people out of their life savings before he was caught," I sighed. "Nobody liked him. They barely even tolerated me."

"So you know why he left," Wolf said gently.

I shrugged.

"Rationally, I do," I said. "But it doesn't change how I feel. I can't control the way I feel."

Wolf started to run his fingers through my hair, and my traitorous body yielded to him and his ministrations.

"Each time he came home, he came to see me, but I refused," I pursed my lips. "I was—and still am—stubborn as hell. It hurt...still hurts."

He snorted. "I could've told you that."

I nipped at his beard and pulled, causing him to laugh.

"Ouch!" He pulled back. "You billy-goated me!"

"Why do you think I did it?" I asked him. "And you just quoted a Ryan Reynolds movie."

"Hmmm," he said. "You're going to give your brother a chance to explain. You're going to give him the time he deserves."

"And how do you know that?" I asked.

"Because you wouldn't be the woman I fell in love with if you didn't."

He was right. I would give Raphael the time. Eventually. Maybe tomorrow or the next day.

Whatever.

I'd do it. I may not be happy about it, but I'd do it.

It was going to be hard for Raphael to bridge this gap between us. I was so hurt, I still am, but Wolf was right, I'd give him the chance to explain.

Because, from what I'd heard Wolf explaining tonight, he'd offered up quite a bit of information about the situation Wolf and I were in.

He'd also given me my dog.

A dog who'd been a great friend since the moment I'd found him. A dog who was trained to protect me, and that wasn't cheap.

My brother, in his own way, had done what he could to watch over me even when I'd refused any contact with and all help from him.

And I found that I quite liked that. Even though I shut him out, he still found a way to try to be there for me. He didn't give up.

My mind raced as my body calmed.

Lani Lynn Vale

CHAPTER 20

Why is life so much like a game of Monopoly? Nobody ever reads the rules until a fight breaks out.
-Fact of life

Wolf

Sated and comfortable for the first time in twelve straight hours, I closed my eyes and pulled my woman closer into my chest.

My hand went to my name that had a new permanent home on Raven's hip, and a surge of pure possessiveness spread through me once again.

"Goddamn, I like having my name on your skin," I told her again, pressing my lips to the back of her neck and dragging them along the length of her shoulder.

She shivered as goosebumps raised over her skin.

"Stop touching me, I'm trying to go to sleep. I have to be at work by eight tomorrow morning." She slapped my hand which was inching up the length of her torso.

I paused just beneath her bare breast and squeezed.

"I…" I was interrupted by the ringing of my phone from my discarded pants pocket, and it took everything I had in me to roll over and let her go.

"Damn it all to hell," I muttered as I let Raven go and reached for my pants.

Raven rolled and buried her face into my pillow, presenting me with her back.

Peeling my eyes away from Raven's backside, I answered the phone.

"Yeah?" I asked.

When nothing came, I growled in frustration.

"Dammit, Goody. If you're not going to talk, why did you call?" I asked the stupid fucker.

"H-how do you always know it's me?"

Because you're stupid and call from the same gas station phone every single time you call me.

I didn't tell him that, though. I liked knowing when it was him.

Sometimes I didn't want to deal with his shit.

"Goody," I sighed. "What do you need?"

"I think I need you to bring your friends. I just saw some girl get shot and thrown into the water."

I stiffened and immediately stood, dislodging Raven's legs from mine.

"Goody, where are you?" I asked him, grabbing my pants.

Raven ripped them from my hands and shoved the leg holes back where they belonged, then tossed me a pair of underwear while she untangled the belt and the gun from the waistband.

"I'm at the diner," he whispered, fear shaking his voice.

I stood up from putting my underwear on, and immediately grabbed the pants that Raven was holding out for me.

"The diner. I'll be there," I tried for calm. "I'm going to stay on the line with you, okay?"

My eyes connected with Raven, and I gave her a nod of thanks.

"No, he said at the diner," Raven was saying into her phone. "Didn't say much else. He's freaked out."

Raven picked up a shirt of mine that she'd been wearing earlier, and I slipped it on over my head, holding the phone away from my face just long enough to get it into place. She continued to dress herself in between helping me.

In that half a second, though, something happened, and the last thing I heard was Goody screaming.

"Fuck me," I growled when the line went dead.

"Which do you want?" Raven asked as she held up two options.

I pointed at my boots and sat down on the bed and quickly shoved my feet into socks she left on the bed for me, adrenaline pumping through my entire body.

Goody wasn't anything much to me, but he was a fucking person.

He was a human being who really had no business doing what he was doing, but a human being nonetheless.

"Is anyone on their way to you?" I asked Raven.

"Yes," she said. "Mig, I think."

I nodded my head.

I stuffed my feet into my boots, holstered my gun into my belt, and then hooked on my badge that was sitting on the bed beside my phone and keys.

Once everything was in place, I had Raven finish dressing and placed my spare gun down the waistband of her jeans. I took her hand and led her down the hallway.

"Wolf," she said, already protesting. "I don't think it's necessary that I go in there."

I stopped outside of the panic room door.

"You can come out when Mig gets here," I told her, holding her face in my hands. "You'll see him on the monitors."

"Mig…"

I shook my head.

"I lost my wife. My kid. Please, don't fight me on this. I know how fucked up people are, and they won't care that you're an innocent. They'll see you as my woman, and they'll take advantage of that," I hesitated. "I really don't want to come home to you shot in the head like my wife was. I wouldn't recover from that."

She closed her eyes, then turned without another word and punched the code into the panel behind the photo that hung on the wall next to the door.

When I had this house built, that'd been the first thing that I told the builder I needed.

The builder had gone above and beyond, leaving me with a room that no one, not even the president himself, could get into.

Not if I didn't want them to, anyway.

"Be careful," Raven whispered as she backed into the room.

I nodded my head. "I will be."

That was the last thing I ever said to her as the man I once was.

CHAPTER 21

*Life isn't about moments that take your breath away. It could be
you're thinking of asthma.*
-Note to self

Wolf

The ride to the boat that I had docked at the Uncertain Saints
clubhouse was harrowing at best.

It was raining, the lightning kept fucking with my night vision, and
my goddamned hand was killing me from my earlier activities that
had my fist visiting Raphael's face.

Despite my fist meeting his face, Raphael knew he had it coming.

I didn't like being worried about my woman, and he could've fixed
a lot of these things that were broken a long fucking time ago by
just opening his fucking mouth.

He didn't, however.

He let me figure it out on my own time, and by the time I did that,
I'd nearly gotten myself killed.

Agent Josh Fry was a sick motherfucker.

I found this out tonight when Raphael spilled absolutely everything
he knew.

And everything he knew was a shitload of trouble that I didn't need nor want in my town.

Luckily, we'd gotten the cameras set up tonight thanks to Mig and Casten, which also meant whatever had gone down tonight with Goody, and whomever he saw, was on camera.

My phone rang in my pocket and I answered it, which was a no-no when I didn't have a hand to spare, but I did it anyway.

"Yeah?" I yelled loudly over the hum of the engine.

"You know," Peek said.

"I know a little bit," I offered. "Goody called me with information about a woman being killed and thrown into the river. I was on the phone with him when he screamed and the line went dead."

"That's what I got, too," Peek said. "I have Xavier with me, and he's telling me that he found something."

"What did he find when he wasn't supposed to be involved anymore?" I asked through gritted teeth as I pulled up to the clubhouse.

"Come pick me up," Peek said. "Talk to you then."

I pulled onto the side of the parking lot and shoved my phone into my pocket before turning the truck off.

Placing my keys under the seat, I jogged down the path that led to the water, cursing when I saw the water had risen since last time I'd been there.

"Fucking rain," I growled, wading into the water up to my knees before I got to the boat. "Fucking fuck."

Climbing into the boat, I was just about to push off when a bike rode in from my back.

I stopped and waited, unsurprised to find Griffin jogging toward me.

He hit the water with a rush and trudged up to me as if the water didn't affect him in the least.

"Go," Griffin said.

A man of many words Griffin was not.

I went and was glad that I had the backup.

How he knew, I didn't know, but I'd take it.

I'd called the cops on the way there, but that wasn't to say that Ridley had enough time to talk to any of the members when he was likely on the way to the scene himself.

We didn't speak until Peek got into the boat with us, and by the time we were heading full throttle toward the diner, I was beyond pissed.

"Tell me what's going on," I said to Peek as we rode.

"The kid came over around eleven saying that he hacked into the FBI database and did a search for Agent Fry. Lots of shit going down tonight according to a live feed that he was able to hack into between Fry and another agent." He pulled out his phone. "Then I go to look at the cameras that we have on the diner and see this going down."

I watched as Agent Fry with his ice-cold eyes picked the woman up by her neck, held her over the water, and then shot her in the forehead with the gun that was on his hip.

The moment her body went limp, he let her fall, not caring in the least that she was likely to show up further down river.

The mother fucker thought he was invincible.

I took a turn around the bend of the river, and was surprised to find Core waving me down.

I pulled up next to him and shut the engine off.

"I have a back way in there. Tie your boat off and get into mine."
He pointed at a dock.

I tied the boat off and moved into his.

Peek and Griffin followed suit, and soon we were underway again,
through thick shrubs and trees.

Core's boat was made to do this, though.

Being a game warden meant that Core had to go places that
weren't always conventional, and he had the boat that was
practically made for anything his job could spring on him.

"Whose dock is this?" I asked him as we started moving slowly
away from the bank.

"Another game warden," he answered once we passed the dock
and my boat. "This is a boat road that was closed down about
twenty years ago because a bald eagle nest was spotted in the area.
The boat road leads us to within about a quarter mile of the diner.
I'm thinking since the water's up so high, we should be able to
make it without coming right on in with the rest of the general
population."

I nodded my head, but my cup half empty nature reared his head.

"What do we do if we can't get there?"

Core smiled.

"I have a dinghy."

"You have a dinghy," I replied blandly.

"Sounds kinky," Griffin offered his two cents.

I rolled my eyes.

And twenty minutes later, four grown ass adults all two hundred
plus pounds, shoved into Core's fucking dinghy and paddled the
last five hundred yards to our worst nightmares.

***

We arrived to a quiet diner.

Nothing was out of place. No boats were in the open.

Nothing.

Not a damn thing.

"Well, what now?" I asked the other three men with me.

"Shh," Core pointed. "There're lights in the diner."

We paddled our way up to the tiny sliver of grass that surrounded the diner and got out.

"Push it into the bushes," I pointed. "It's black and won't be seen unless they're actively looking for it."

Core pushed the boat into the bushes at the same time I started making my way around the building.

I went for the kitchen entrance instead of the front or back entrance, thinking that it was the better choice.

It wasn't.

And I didn't find that out until I got a belly full of birdshot blasted from a shotgun the moment I made my way stealthily around the corner.

Apparently, my thinking I was stealthy and actually being stealthy were two different things.

Luck was on my side, though.

The man that shot was too far away, meaning instead of getting shot straight into my stomach, the shot had time to spread and slow.

My belly still had birdshot embedded in it, but instead of being buried deep, it was buried shallowly, not having penetrated past the first layer of skin.

Ducking down and rolling into the water, I surfaced ten feet away from where I'd previously been, and came up shooting.

The man went down, taking one shot by me, and one shot by Peek who'd followed me around.

I shook the water from my face and started to trudge out of the water.

"Fuckin' A, man," I grumbled, lifting up my shirt to see my belly.

There were no lights, though, and I couldn't see a damn thing.

I felt it, though, that was for sure.

We breached the kitchen door moments later, and came to a sudden standstill when we found the kitchen full.

Not with men, but with women.

***

Thirty minutes later, I was still just as surprised as I was when I'd entered the room.

"Do we have a story that's been confirmed by more than two women?" I asked Griffin.

Griffin shook his head.

"Fuck no." Griffin took off his hat and ran his fingers through his hair.

I'd lost my hat about five minutes into the fiasco I'd dubbed *Project: What the fuck.*

When we'd entered the diner thirty minutes ago, it was to find over fifty women in the room.

The diner was set up like one large room. From the front door where you entered, you could see the back door, the side door that entered the kitchen, and the area that led to the men's and women's bathrooms.

There was a large bar that separated the kitchen from the rest of the room where patrons were more than welcome to sit, and then there were about twenty tables scattered sporadically throughout the room.

And every one of those tables had women occupying them.

All of them were in various stages of dress.

Most were dressed in little more than rags, almost as if when they'd been taken, they'd been in bed.

Others were in jeans and t-shirts. Some short sleeves, others long. Which, in my mind, meant that they'd come from different areas of the country. It hadn't been cold enough in the last month and a half to warrant snow boots like some of the women were wearing.

Still, others were in fucking dresses and heels.

Every single woman looked tired and in need of a bath, and they all were scared.

And there was a sleeper among them, which was why they were still shoved in this fucking diner instead of on their way to a police station somewhere where they could be questioned and then released.

I don't know what was telling me that there was someone here that was potentially harmful.

All I knew was that there were two armed men outside patrolling the perimeter, a missing man with—get this—strange, eerie blue eyes, and not a single person inside that was there to watch and keep control of the situation.

Yeah, I wasn't born yesterday.

"Separate them by amount of time. Start by questioning the women who've been held the longest and ask them about the new arrivals first. Use the women to check each other," I ordered.

Ridley, who'd shown up at the end of my order, nodded his head in agreement.

"I'm in agreement with you, though. It doesn't make sense that they would've left all those women in here by themselves. Someone was keeping them in check on the inside, and we haven't found that person yet. We can't just let them go until we know who that person is," he agreed.

After we separated, I found myself with a woman who looked like she was trying to crawl into herself.

"Ma'am," I cleared my throat. "Do you mind if I ask you a few questions?"

The simple act of coming up behind her made her jolt in her seat and practically throw herself onto the floor to get away from me.

Knowing that I wouldn't get a damn thing out of her if she was that scared of me, I backed up and put about five feet in between us.

"I'm sorry," I said.

"Wolf?" someone called.

I turned and found a female sheriff's deputy calling my name, and a smiling Hannah beside her.

"What are you doing here?" I asked her as I moved away from the woman and toward the other two.

"They asked any available medical professionals that had any triage knowledge to volunteer to come out here. Me and a couple of other women from the hospital came to help. Where do you want me?" she asked.

I turned to look at the room at large.

There was no way in hell that I was going to just let her go wherever the hell she wanted to go, and then my eyes lit on Travis who'd done his level best to stay the hell away from me throughout the entire ordeal.

An all-available-personnel had been sent out to the towns that surrounded Uncertain, and any and all help that was available had come. Since Travis was a reserve police officer two towns over, he came.

He didn't like that it was me that he came for, though, and he'd made known that he wanted nothing to do with me.

So he'd given me a wide berth, and I'd let him have it.

I'd trust him with Hannah's life, though, and since all of my brothers were busy, he'd be the next best thing as an extension of me. The female officer wasn't a good fit either; she was needed to keep some of the women calm—like the scared chick who I'd tried to approach earlier.

"Come with me," I said to Hannah, nodding my head at the deputy in thanks. "I have someone that'll watch over you while you work."

My mind, however, was on a few people who, suspiciously, weren't here.

Like Agent Josh fucking Fry, who I knew for a fact was in the fucking area.

How fucking convenient.

"Who are you making my babysitter?" Hannah asked with mirth-filled eyes, taking me away from my contemplations.

I looked at her, then back over to Travis, who saw me coming and stiffened.

His eyes flicked over to Hannah—and surprise—he liked what he saw.

That made me want to laugh.

Travis was a chick hater like Mig used to be—only worse.

He despised all women, but his sister and Raven, since I'd known him.

I'd never been let in on why exactly he was such a prick to anything with a vagina, but knowing that Hannah affected him in some way really had me choking back a comical laugh at the situation.

Fucker deserved to have a woman upset his tidy little world—and it made me fucking happy as hell that Hannah was the one who got that kind of reaction out of him.

"Travis," I said, stopping a few feet in front of him. "This is Hannah, she's one of my good friends who is here to help ascertain if any of these ladies are in need of medical attention. Hannah, this is Travis Hail. Do either one of you need anything from me?"

A shake of both of their heads had me grinning as I turned and walked away, my belly smarting as I turned wrong.

I'd been looked over by a paramedic earlier and had seven pellets removed from my belly. All of them were less than a quarter inch into my skin. After getting a dose of antibiotics and my wounds cleaned, I was sent on my way.

That didn't mean that it didn't still hurt like fuck.

"Yo," Peek called as I made my way back to the woman I was going to question before Hannah showed up.

Stopping, I turned in the direction of where Peek was. A woman was at his side, holding her arm across her chest as if she were trying to keep as much distance in between us as she could and still appear as if she was cooperating.

"What's up?" I asked him once I arrived.

Peek's eyes caught mine and something inside of me came to attention.

He didn't have to say a damn word and I understood. That was the nature of such a close brotherhood like The Uncertain Saints had, though.

"This is Annelise," he said. "She's got a few things she thinks you may need to hear. Maybe out of the way of all these ladies."

I nodded my head and gestured to the kitchen area—which happened to be across the room—that gave as much privacy as we were going to get in this big open room.

She stiffly walked at my side, keeping as much distance between us as she could while we made our way in the direction of the kitchen.

It wasn't the way she moved at my side that alerted me to the possible problem.

No, it was the way that every single woman in the room moved out of her way. Not overly scared, but wary. Almost as if the woman had given them a reason to be scared of her.

I realized the problem at the same time that she did, and that's when she produced a pistol from her front and brandished it, pointing it straight at my head.

Where she'd stowed it, I didn't know. At that point, though, it didn't matter.

I moved like lightning, and it still wasn't enough.

How some small woman, who was barely five foot anything could get the drop on me, I didn't know, but she did.

One second I was walking at her side, my hand at her mid-back as I guided her to where I wanted her, and the next she was shooting me in the head.

I had enough time to move, but not enough to keep me from getting shot.

Lucky for me, I was able to drop and throw my body at her, which threw off her aim. Going from the middle of my face to the top of my head.

I went down, but I took the bitch with me.

CHAPTER 22

Shut up, I wear heels bigger than your dick.
-Raven's secret thoughts

Raven

I stared at the cameras, hoping beyond hope that what I was seeing wasn't what I was seeing.

But the man shifted again, and Nathan, Wolf's baby boy, shifted with him.

His eyes were closed and he looked like he was dead.

Mig was nowhere to be seen and hadn't shown in the hour and a half that I'd been in here, and now I was staring at one of my worst nightmares.

The only thing that was keeping me slightly calm was the fact that it was my brother who had Nathan and not the creepy guy beside him.

"Come out, come out, wherever you are!" the creepy fucker called, looking directly into the camera as if he knew I was there watching him.

I wanted to knock him in the face with my knee.

And I would.

As soon as I had Nathan safe.

Knowing this might turn out to bite me in the ass, I fired off a text to Wolf, Mig, Peek, and Alison, and then centered myself.

Going against everything inside me that screamed for me to stay put, I unlocked the door using the code that Wolf had given me a few weeks ago and hurried straight toward the front door where I knew they were.

I yanked open the door without checking to see if anyone was there, and came face-to-face with one of my worst nightmares.

"What did you do to him?" I hissed, reaching for Nathan.

My brother—who'd never so much as looked at me like he knew me—handed Nathan over as if that was what he intended to do all along. Almost as if he were just dropping him off from spending the day with him.

Nathan settled in my arms and then wrapped himself around me like he always did, only sleepier.

Raphael's eyes were blank as he stared at me. The other man's, however, were not.

They were full of mirth as he reached for my hand.

"Come," he pushed me into the house and followed behind me.

Raphael followed him, and then shut the door. The lock clicking shut was the loudest thing I'd ever heard.

"Who are y'all?" I backed up until my back was to the wall.

Everything inside of me was practically shaking in terror. On the outside, I was as cool as a cucumber, or at least I hoped I was anyway.

Nathan shifted until his face was against my neck, his hot breath breathing out against my skin with a little snore at the end that would've been adorable had we not been in this rather terrifying situation.

My eyes went to the gun on my brother's hip and then went back to the other man who had a gun underneath his shoulder.

"We're with the FBI," the pale blue-eyed man said, sounding sickeningly sweet as he did. "We're here to inform you that something has happened to your boyfriend."

My brows furrowed, and I immediately moved my gaze from the blue-eyed man to my brother.

My brother gave an almost imperceptible shake of his head, and I realized that my instincts weren't steering me wrong.

They were, in fact, telling me that I should be scared. That this man wasn't who he said he was.

Sure, he may actually be with the FBI, but there was no reason on Earth that Nathan should be brought here if there was something wrong with Wolf.

First, his grandmother would be the one to call me had they contacted her, and second, everyone in the town knew that Wolf and I were together. Ridley was the law around these parts, and the man was Wolf's brother. *He* would come to tell me. What he would not do was let some man that had no connection to me whatsoever come to me.

He would *not* go get Nathan, at least not without Wolf's or my permission first.

So no, I wasn't falling for this man's bullshit that he was shoveling.

"What happened to him?" I asked, letting the fear and worry that I was feeling fill my voice. "Is he okay?"

The man walked forward until his hand was resting on Nathan's back. "He is right now…" he smiled at me, letting me see those freaky eyes up close. "But he won't be for long."

I stiffened and tried to turn my body to get the man's hand away from Nathan, but when I moved, the man smiled and tightened his hand until his fist was wrapped around Nathan's shirt.

"I want you to call him."

I nodded my head.

"Okay," I said. "I'll call him."

He grinned at me.

"You'll use my phone."

I nodded again.

I didn't want the man to follow me into the safe room. That was a secret, and if he knew about it, it wasn't so secret or safe anymore, was it?

"Okay," I said. "But I don't know Wolf's number."

I didn't. He'd put it into my phone when I'd first met him, and then I'd never thought twice about calling him after that. How stupid was it that I didn't know that?

Hell, I didn't know anyone's number…except for one.

And my brother was standing right there, so there was no way in hell I could call him.

"That's okay," the man smiled. "Rafe here knows it."

That didn't surprise me.

Was Rafe playing a bad guy?

I knew a little bit about what he was doing, just that he was undercover and involved in some big investigation that Wolf was also somehow involved in.

Whether this was the same man he was investigating, I didn't know.

But I did want to know, and I would know. Soon.

Now, though, I decided to go ahead and use the pale blue-eyed man to call Wolf and let him know that I thought something fishy was going on.

"Rafe, the number," the man asked, snapping his fingers.

"Alright, Fry. Simmer down," he ordered, pulling out his phone.

He rattled off a number, and this Fry guy punched in the numbers and pressed dial before putting it onto speakerphone.

"'Lo?" Wolf's angry, pain-filled voice answered.

"Hi, Wolf. This is Agent Fry, here to check on your lovely lady and child like you asked me to," he called jovially into the phone.

"Raven?" Wolf asked softly. Carefully.

"Yes, Wolf?" I asked, knowing when he was mad.

And mad wouldn't even touch what he was feeling right now. He was pissed. Hot. So angry he would be vibrating had he been near me.

"You don't follow directions," he said, sounding almost bored.

"No," I agreed. "But Agent Fry brought Nathan over here to me with another man. He said you were hurt."

Before Wolf could reply, Agent Fry took the phone away from me and placed it to his ear, turning away from the two of us and letting me see my brother for the first time.

Raphael's face went from passive to angry in the half a second since I'd last looked at him.

I raised my eyebrow at him in question and shifted Nathan in my arms.

"Where's Nancy?" I whispered.

Raphael's eyes went haunted, and the shake of his head said it all.

Nancy wasn't good.

Whatever happened to her to get Nathan with me had been bad, and I prayed that whatever was wrong with her that she would be able to recover from it.

"Search her, Rafe," Agent Fry called over his shoulder. "Make sure she doesn't have anything on her that she can use against us in the next ten minutes that it takes Wolf to arrive."

"What's going on?" I asked carefully.

Agent Fry's crazy eyes came to me, and he smiled. A smile so fucking chilling that I felt the ice all the way across the room.

"What's going on is that I'm about to kill your man, and you're going to watch."

And suddenly I wasn't standing with my back to the wall anymore. Suddenly, I had my brother's hands running down the length of my arms and legs as he searched for anything I would be able to use against them.

My brother did a shit job though. He skimmed right over my cell phone. Let me hold on to the set of keys that were in my pocket—a set of keys that had a deadly and wicked keychain on them that was meant to shove into people's eyes.

He also skipped over the gun. The same gun that Wolf had placed in the back of my pants before he'd left.

At the time, I'd thought he was being overzealous.

Now, though, I was understanding just how right he'd been to worry.

"She's clean," he said. "Where do you want us to go?"

"Put the kid in their room. Both of you come out here."

"If the kid wakes up, he's going to be scared since we took him from his grandmother's. I propose we stay in the backroom while you await Wolf," Raphael said, gesturing behind him at Nathan.

My arms tightened involuntarily, and I realized I was doing a lot better at this than I would have been had Raphael not been here.

And I realized something; in the middle of whatever bullshit that I was in, I trusted my brother.

Meaning I knew he'd take care of me and not let anything happen to me.

Surely if I trusted him with my life, I could trust him with my heart again.

Agent Fry's eyes came to where Nathan was resting, and then back to me.

"Fine, whatever. At least the fuckin' dog isn't here," he mumbled. "But make sure you keep an eye on her. She's likely a flight risk. Fuck!" Marky Mark was at the clubhouse. Had been there since this afternoon when Alison had picked him up from the groomer's. *Thank God.* I had a feeling if he'd been here, he would be dead right now. He ran his hands through his hair. "Do you know how fucking hard it's going to be to get another shipment in on such short notice?" He licked his lips. "Fifty-seven fucking girls! I had buyers for most of them!"

Raphael pushed me back toward the back hallway of Wolf's house; I started backing up, sensing when to cut and run.

"Be back," Raphael said as he guided me out of the room.

I went willingly.

The moment the door shut, I whirled on him.

"What the fuck is going on?" I hissed at him.

Raphael held his hand up to stop me before I could get too animated about what was going on, and shoved me in the direction of the safe room. Wolf had explained about the safe room in an earlier conversation, apparently.

"Get back in there," he ordered. "I want you to lock it and not open it. Not for any goddamn reason. Not for me getting my head blown off. Not for Wolf getting his blown off either. Not for any goddamn reason. Do you understand?"

I swallowed, a ball of fear keeping me from breathing correctly.

"Yes," I whispered.

"Good. Go. Don't come back out."

With that, he pushed me in the direction of the door to the safe room, and gestured with his fingers for me to hurry up.

Punching in the numbers, I pushed the door open, and Raphael closed the door hard behind me.

Nathan's big body stirred, and I looked down at him when he lifted his face from my shoulder.

"Rave?" he whispered. "Tired."

"Yeah, baby. Go back to sleep."

His face scrunched up and then he nodded his head before laying his head back against my shoulder.

By this point, my hands were aching uncontrollably, and I had to put him down or I'd drop him.

He was a big boy. Way bigger than any kid in his class or on his baseball team.

As I laid him down on the bed that was covered with a scratchy gray blanket, I looked down at him and wondered what in the hell I was supposed to do now.

Was I supposed to just wait here and see what would happen?

Would I need to call the cops?

I had worked myself into a fine hysteric, going from looking at the monitors on the walls that showed me Wolf's house to Nathan's sleeping face, and was nearly convinced to call the cops when I realized that I still had my cell phone. Meaning I could call Wolf.

Jesus Christ!

Nabbing my cell phone, I pressed Wolf's name and put it up to my ear.

It only took him five seconds to answer it, and by the time he did, I could tell he was on his way.

"Raven?" he answered urgently.

"I'm okay. I'm in the safe room."

"Nathan?"

"He's with me," I replied soothingly. "We're okay. Raphael and that guy, Fry, they wanted Nathan away from us. Raphael was able to talk him into putting me in the bedroom with him."

"Who's there with you?"

"Nobody but Raphael and that Fry guy," I whispered. "Wolf…what the heck is going on?"

My eyes went to the bedroom where Raphael was wearing a hole in the floor from his pacing and went back to Nathan's still form.

"Fuck," he whispered, sounding relieved. "That's good to know. I'm on my way. We'll be there in less than five minutes."

I bit my lip. "So what do you want me to do?"

Wolf made a soothing sound.

"Handle what you need to handle in that room. DO whatever you need to do, but do not, under any circumstance, leave that room," he ordered.

That being the second time I was ordered not to leave, I understood doubly well that I was not to leave. If the two main men in my life thought I shouldn't, then I wouldn't.

No way in hell.

"Okay," I agreed. "I'll stay in the room."

"Good." He took a deep breath and the sound of a motor started in the distance. "You may see something you don't like on those videos; I'm asking you to turn the monitors off until you hear the special knock I showed you on the door earlier."

I pursed my lips.

"Wolf..." I started, but he stopped me with one word.

"Please?"

I swallowed thickly.

"Just don't get shot in the head. I'll be good."

Little did I know that I wouldn't have to worry about that one, mainly because the damn man had *already* been shot in the head once tonight.

***

It took Wolf fifteen minutes to arrive, and the moment he did, Raphael alerted me that he was there.

I watched the screen avidly as I waited for Wolf to ride up on his Harley.

At first, I thought he'd gotten a new helmet, but the longer I looked, the more I realized that what he had wrapped around his head wasn't a helmet at all, but a bandage. A black bandage that resembled vet wrap or Cobain.

I leaned forward until my nose was practically touching the screen, and smiled when I saw the men pull up beside him.

Griffin was on one side of him, and Peek on the other.

I had no doubt that the others were on their way.

And they didn't disappoint. By the time Wolf made it to the front door, every single one of the members pulled up behind him.

All except one, and that one, Mig, worried me.

He was supposed to be here over an hour ago, and he still wasn't here.

On a whim, I picked up my phone and found Annie's number, and then hit send as I watched what was happening in front of me.

"Hello?" Annie asked breathlessly.

"Annie?" I asked urgently. "Is everything alright?"

"No!" Annie wailed. "Oh, God. The kid, Xavier…" she hesitated. "He tried to kill himself tonight. Peek must've left Mig's information or something, because Xavier called and told Mig that he was scared. That he tried to kill himself, and had swallowed an entire bottle of pills from the cookie jar in the kitchen. The one that is filled with Vicodin."

My belly rolled as I remembered Wolf showing me that cookie jar.

I looked down at my still-casted hand, the one that just a few weeks ago I'd broken for the first time in my life.

Now the cast was an ugly shade of pink that showed every single speck of dirt, drop of blood, and frayed gauze from where I'd tried to itch the inside of my arm with a coat hanger.

"Oh, God." I whispered. "Is he okay?"

"Yes," Annie sniffled. "But Mig and I are with him in the ER. He's having his stomach pumped right now."

Deciding not to burden her with any more information on what was going on, I said, "Keep me updated, okay? I have Nathan and it's not going to be easy to get to the ER to see him until the morning."

Annie murmured something in agreement, and then said, "Gotta go. I'll keep you informed."

As she hung up, I saw Wolf make his way into the main room, and groaned when I got my first good look at his face that wasn't obscured by shadows.

He was covered (and when I say covered, I mean *fucking Carrie covered*) in blood. It was caked on the skin of his neck. Between the webbing of his fingers. The gray t-shirt he was wearing was saturated. His jeans were a dark shade of blue when I knew for a fact he left in jeans that were so fucking faded that they appeared white.

His hair was sticking up in every freakin direction, and his beard was stiff and straight instead of bushy and neat like he usually kept it.

"What are you doing in my house?" he asked. "Where is my kid and woman?"

Raphael came out of the bedroom and Wolf stiffened, playing the role of a surprised man perfectly.

"What are y'all doing here? Where's Nathan and Raven?" he snarled.

I watched as men started pouring inside of the house, flanking Wolf's back, and staring at the man in front of them like the crazy loon he was.

"You're outnumbered, Fry. Put down the gun and get the fuck out of here," Wolf said. "Maybe try not to point your gun at the sheriff who's in the room."

Fry didn't move the gun he was pointing at Wolf's face.

Raphael, however, chose that moment to pull his own gun out.

He made an arc, swinging it high over the Uncertain Saints heads, and then aimed it directly at the rogue agent that was so screwed in the head.

To even consider the fact that he had a fair chance at accomplishing what he came here to accomplish was surprising to say the least.

What was more surprising was the grin he leveled on Raphael.

"I fucking knew it!" he cried. "I knew you weren't really mine!"

Raphael grinned.

"Yeah," he said. "I've never been yours."

Agent Fry's eyes went absolutely electric. "That's why I have a fail safe."

"And what is that fail safe?" my brother asked him.

"Always carry it around with me," he said, opening his shirt.

All the men in the room, including my brother, stiffened.

"You're going to die," Wolf snapped, taking a step forward. "Are you fucking crazy?"

The angle the cameras were at, and where the men were positioned, kept me from seeing what he pulled out of his shirt and had in his hand.

The men, though, had absolutely no trouble seeing what Fry wanted them to see.

And when they started backing up, I knew whatever Fry was holding was serious.

Deadly serious.

And then Wolf's shoulders moved, giving me my first good view of what was in his hand.

"Oh, fuck."

I pulled my phone back up, dialed 9-1-1, and then placed it to my ear.

"9-1-1, what's your emergency?" the man asked.

Quickly I spouted off where we were, but I couldn't give them the exact address because I didn't know. I vowed right then and there that when I survived this, and I would fucking survive this, I was going to memorize Wolf's number and fucking address.

"A man is in our house with a grenade," I whispered, even though the men in the room beyond me had no chance of hearing what I had to say. "He pulled the pin, and there are seven men in the room beside the man with the grenade. Two are Texas Rangers, one is the sheriff. He's going to kill all of them if he drops that grenade."

Then, to my horror, Fry threw the grenade at the men.

In reaction to the thing flying at their heads—whether it be live or fake—they all scattered.

All the men moved at once as a unit.

They weren't fast enough, though.

Not nearly fast enough.

CHAPTER 23

You don't have to be crazy to be my friend. It'll happen on its own…just give it time.
-Wolf's secret thoughts

Wolf

"You can't go!" Hannah cried. "You've got a gunshot wound to your head!"

I pushed off the gurney where I'd been placed when I passed out, and stood up on my own two feet.

"What's going on?" Peek asked.

"Fry's at my place. With Raven and Nathan."

The entire room went wired at the mention of that.

"Where's Mig?" Peek asked.

I shook my head.

"I'm afraid to ask," I admitted.

Core appeared and gestured to me, and I took the moment of confusion between everyone to slip out past Hannah, who was arguing with Griffin and Peek.

Peek followed me with Griffin following him.

Core and Casten were somewhere behind them, and together as a unit, we exited the diner and made our way to Core's boat which was brought around by one of the police officers.

With my heart in my throat, we made our way as fast as Core's boat would take us to where we'd left our vehicles.

My heart was pounding a million miles an hour and not just because of the blood loss.

My cell phone rang, and I breathed a sigh of relief when I saw who was calling.

"Raven."

I woke up, heart pounding as I relived my worst nightmare. Again.

"Raven!" I cried. "Nathan!"

"Shhh," Peek said, his Irish brogue causing me to turn my head to the side to see him.

He looked banged up as hell, and there was something wrong with his right arm.

My eyes slid down the sling to the neon green cast that was encasing his arm.

"What the fuck?" I breathed, voice raw.

It felt like I'd smoked a pack of cigarettes, and all I could smell was smoke.

My head was pounding, and I was fairly sure I couldn't feel my feet.

Was it normal to feel like you were floating?

Peek reached forward and pressed a red button beside my bed, and sweet soothing relief started to flow through me.

"They're okay," Peek said softly. "Everyone is okay."

My eyes closed.

"Okay," I said. "Fucking great."

My eyes closed of their own volition

***

Raven

I swallowed as I looked in on Nancy, smiling as she talked softly to her grandson about why her eye was black.

"That horse just jumped up and caught me good, right in the noggin," she said to him.

I backed out of the room, thankful that she was okay, and waved at her granddaughter as I left.

Her granddaughter waved back, and I closed the door firmly before rounding the corner and heading to the next room.

I was making my rounds.

Six of the seven members of The Uncertain Saints MC were in the hospital, and five of them had been admitted.

Peek and Mig being the only two who weren't occupying a hospital bed, five rooms in a row.

Then there were Nancy and Xavier, although they weren't Uncertain Saints, who were also occupying the same floor.

It was like a fuckin' reunion for the sickly.

"Everything okay?" I asked Annie, who was standing outside Xavier's room.

"Yes," she breathed. "How about yours?"

I nodded my head. "Wolf's still in and out. Nancy is awake and talking. Apparently, she never saw a thing that happened. She woke up on the floor with her granddaughter standing over her."

Annie breathed out roughly. "Xavier told us that he got an email from his father, except it wasn't his father, it was Agent Fry sending him a picture of his father who was dead."

"Goddammit" I growled. "That guy needs to fucking die."

Annie nodded her head in agreement. "Peek was released and is in Wolf's room from last I heard," she said. "And the rest of the ladies are in the rooms with their men. All have received the green light that they can go home after they're sure the concussions haven't done any damage."

My head dropped and I rubbed the back of my neck.

"My brother's about two seconds away from checking himself out AMA," I said. "Against medical advisement. Seriously. I don't know what's wrong with him."

"There's nothing wrong with him," my brother said from behind me, dressed in street clothes that I had no earthly idea how he got by himself when he could barely stand up straight."

All of the men had concussions. All had at least one broken bone. Wolf, however, being the hero of the group, had the worst of all the injuries.

He had a broken arm to match my broken arm. He had a broken tibia. Seven broken ribs. Burns on twenty percent of his body. A concussion. A shot to the head that they were watching closely. Gunshot wounds to his belly. Oh, and he had a kidney injury that they were watching closely due to a concussion blast when the grenade went off.

"What do you think you're doing?" I asked him, putting myself between him and Annie, which also happened to be me putting myself between him and the exit of the floor.

"I'm going down to the county jail."

"Why?" I asked.

"Because I'm looking to make a better acquaintance with ex-agent Josh Fry."

I grinned.

"You won't find him at the jail," I said. "Mig got to him before the cops could. Said it was his jurisdiction, and that was that."

"Hmmm," Raphael said, grin getting larger. "That's too bad for him."

"I need your help."

My brother, surprised that I was willingly asking him for anything, turned to face me fully.

"Anything."

"If you're bound and determined to see him, I have a favor." I looked over at Annie, then back to Raphael. "I need a ride to where they're holding him."

***

I can't say that the next two hours were among my finest moments.

In fact, I would say they were some of the darkest moments in my life.

Once we'd arrived at the clubhouse, Raphael had worked his magic and got me time with the Uncertain Saints prisoner.

Mig hadn't been willing to give it to me at first, but when Peek showed up two minutes after we'd arrived and told Mig to allow me to have the time, he'd done it. Albeit unwillingly.

And I say prisoner lightly.

He was in the kitchen of the houseboat, plastic sheeting underneath his feet as he sat tied with his hands behind his back.

"Get him up for me. Put him in the seat so I don't have to bend down to see his eyes," I swallowed. "And then leave."

"Raven…" Raphael hesitated. "You know I can't do that."

I raised an eyebrow at him.

"Sure you can," I said. "All you have to do is put him there, and leave. Easy peasy."

He shook his head. "Wolf would literally kill me."

I smiled at him.

"If you do this for me, I'll forgive you. I'll let you back into my life. I'll stop ignoring your calls and texts. Everything you always wanted. Just do this one thing for me," I said pleadingly, knowing he'd do it.

Raphael looked at me, contemplated it for point two five seconds, and then grabbed Josh Fry by his throat, and immediately punched him in the head to knock him out.

My brother's anger and pain seemed to be exponentially larger than I'd thought, and I idly wondered if I should let him stay and witness what I was about to do.

The ex-agent fell to the floor, his eyes rolling into the back of his head.

Once he'd strapped him down to the table, his hands above it and the rest of him securely tied to a chair that was bolted to the floor, he left the room.

I knew he wouldn't go far.

In fact, he was probably watching me.

Raphael tied his arms with a scratchy rope to the table by a loop that was welded in the very middle.

His feet were next, only these were attached to the metal chair itself by a pair of manacles that'd been welded to it.

His head lolled, and I smiled at Raphael to let him know I'd be alright.

"Thank you. You can go."

Raphael clearly didn't want to leave me, but with one look in my eyes, he did so.

"Yell if you need me," he said, and then made his way out of the room before closing the door.

It took ten minutes for Fry to regain consciousness, and in those ten minutes, I'd gathered my supplies.

A groan from behind me had me turning to survey the man.

His eyes trained on me, and it took everything in me not to punch the man's face in.

"What did you think?" I asked the man in front of me. "Did you think that I would just forget that you touched my kid? One who'd done nothing wrong, who was just the child of the man you perceived as a threat to your fucking livelihood?" I stepped forward. "I saw the marks on his chest when I took him to the hospital. Bruises on his ribs from where you kicked him before my brother could stop you."

The man, now ex-agent Josh Fry, sneered at me.

"When the police come, you're going to go to jail for what you're doing."

He knew just as well as I that this wasn't protocol. The law was looking for him, undoubtedly.

"Yeah," I agreed. He was likely right. Would that change what I was about to do? Fuck no. "My brother's been with you for months now. Did you know that?"

"Not until tonight, no," Fry said. "But I knew he wasn't right when he wouldn't fuck the merchandise, which should've been my first clue that something wasn't right." He grinned. "I used to show him pictures of me fucking the women. Some as young as fourteen."

I don't know what came over me.

One second I was staring at the man in front of me who was giving every detail of his last eight years, how he sold hundreds of women to men that purchased them to be used as slaves, and the next I just snapped.

The cleaver that I was sure was for decoration rather than actual use was mounted on the wall over the kitchen sink.

The moment I grabbed it, my body became numb.

Taking the cleaver over to the man—no, filthy scum because the man didn't deserve the title of a man—I reared back, cleaver in hand, and brought it down over the man's tied hands.

It imbedded in his flesh, went all the way to the metal table, and stopped.

Dropping the clever on the table while Fry screamed, I looked at him dispassionately as the door to the room opened.

"Let's see how well you can touch people who don't want your touch with no fuckin' hands."

With that parting comment, I rushed out of the room, past my brother, and straight to the back door.

I made it all the way to the side of the boat before I lost my lunch.

EPILOGUE

If a woman asks if she's fat, there are multiple things you can do in this situation. However, 'no' isn't adequate enough. You must also act surprised that she would even ask that question. As well, you should probably jump back as if she'd just offered you a grievous blow.
-Words of wisdom

Wolf

1 year later

I sat down on the metal bleachers and watched as Nathan came back up to bat.

Marky Mark leaned at my side, content to watch his little friend play.

Nathan looked over at me, grinned widely at seeing me sitting in my normal spot, and turned his head back to the game.

"Elbow up, boy!" I yelled. "Eye on the ball."

Nathan nodded his head and lifted his elbow.

I leaned forward and rested my hands around Raven's shoulders, massaging them as I watched my boy bat.

"He's going to strike out," I muttered. "He can't keep his eyes off of you."

She giggled.

"I'm not normally dressed in a dress," she said. "I can understand why he keeps looking at me like I'm not me."

I chuckled and placed my head on top of hers.

"Strike!" the umpire called loudly.

"Get your head in the game, boy," I told my son, who'd just today turned seven years old. "Watch what you're doing."

Nathan grinned unabashedly and squared his hips to the plate.

The next pitch, thankfully from a pitching machine this year instead of a coach, tossed the ball toward him.

It was the perfect pitch, right in Nathan's sweet spot.

He waited, twitched, and then swung.

The ball and bat connected, and for the second time this season, he hit a homerun.

Only this time it was an in-field home run rather than an out-of-the-park one.

"Run!" I bellowed getting up on my feet and jumping right along with the rest of them.

Marky Mark was on his hind feet, front paws planted on the chain link fence beside me, in the action, too.

"You really shouldn't have come here in that dress," Annie said. "You're going to get it dirty as hell."

Raven shrugged. "Who cares? I'm never going to wear it again after today."

I grinned.

"No, you most certainly will not," I agreed, running my fingers down the delicate slip of a wedding dress. "You, Mrs. Wolfgang Amsel, will be hanging this up and never touching it for the rest of your life. You won't *ever* be needing it again."

Raven tossed me a grin over her shoulder. "I kind of like the sound of that."

"Of what?" Lenore asked as she sat down, Griffin sliding onto the seat beside her. "What's with that look on your face?"

I looked at Raven's face and grinned.

"She's happy to see me," I explained to Lenore. "She didn't think I'd make it in time."

"I thought you'd make it," she said. "You were, however, late to your own wedding and we had to move it to after the baseball game. How is that my fault that I can't wipe the smile off my face?"

"You know that you're not supposed to see her or the dress before the wedding, right?" Tasha asked as she took a seat on my other side, Casten right beside her.

"Yes," I agreed. "But that's a load of bullshit anyway."

"Oh, shit," Hannah said, waddling toward me as fast as she could. "I'm so late. Did she hit yet?"

I grinned at Hannah and her largely pregnant belly.

"No, not yet. You missed Nathan hitting another home run, though," I teased her.

Hannah waved her hand in the air.

"Where's Travis?" I asked.

Hannah's eyes went haunted as she shrugged.

"I came by myself. Shit, my vagina feels like it's going to burst," Hanna supplied as she took a seat. "Just you wait, Raven. This'll be you in a few months."

I froze as I turned my smiling gaze, which dropped from Hannah's face, to Raven's stiffened body.

"Raven," I said carefully.

"What?" Raven squeaked.

"What is she…"

"Hey!" Raphael said, jogging up. "What are you doing looking at my sister? You know that's bad luck."

Raphael took a seat next to Raven on the bleacher below me, and threw his arm around her shoulder.

"Hey, brother," Raven cried, throwing her hand around her brother's waist. "What are you doing here?"

"I'm being deployed," he said. "I needed to come say goodbye before I left, and tell you that I won't be able to make your wedding. Although I would have had you had it on time. Thanks for being late, by the way." He glared at me, then returned his gaze to his sister. "Do you think that we can reschedule our camping trip in two weeks?"

I squeezed Raven's shoulders slightly, causing her to exhale. "Jesus, Hannah. I haven't told him yet. Couldn't you have been more careful?"

Hannah's eyes went wide. "How was I supposed to know? Everyone knows!"

"Everyone but him!" She pointed a finger. "It's your fault you know."

"What?" I asked. "Why my fault?"

"I had it timed perfectly. You were supposed to come in. We get married. Then the photographer was supposed to get on camera me telling you that I'm pregnant," she sighed. "You ruined everything by being late."

"Why does everyone know, then?" I asked.

"She had a man drop it from the sky in a fucking plane. It was epic," Griffin supplied. "Too bad you missed it."

I dropped my head to Raven's. "I'm sorry. I didn't mean to be late."

"It's okay," she lied. "I understand."

"It wasn't my fault, though."

She snorted. "It's never your fault."

I showed her my arm.

"The guy stabbed me with a knife. What did you want me to do? Come to the judge to marry you with my blood running down my arm?" I asked her, showing her my new stitches.

"No," she growled, eyeing the cut. "What I wanted you to do is take a fucking day off from crime fighting. The rest of the men in the club did. So you should've been able to."

I glared at Griffin, who had the nerve to laugh.

"I swear I won't be late to my next wedding."

She pinched the inside of my thigh, and I laughed as I pushed her forward.

"Come with me for a second."

She got up, and I got my first good look at her wedding dress.

"Follow me," I ordered, grabbing her hand.

She tossed her purse down onto the bleachers where she'd been sitting and pointed at Lenore.

"Watch that, will you?" she asked. "It has our rings in it."

I snatched the purse, fished the rings out of it, and tossed it to Griffin, who caught it without taking his eyes off the game in front of him, "Take her car and the dog to our place, will you?"

"Yeah." Griffin grunted, eyes still on the game.

"Where are we going?" she asked as I pulled her along.

"To go get married."

"What?" she cried. "But no one will be there."

"You will. I will," I said as I led her to my bike.

She stared at me like I'd lost my mind.

"What the hell, Wolf?" She tilted her head. "We're gonna miss Nathan's game."

"Nathan's game is nearly over, and they were at the bottom of the inning. They're practically finished."

She shook her head.

"But...why the rush?"

I pulled her until her front rested against mine.

Pressing my throbbing erection into her belly, I made my elation known.

"Because I need to get my ring on your finger."

"Why now? I want pictures!" she said stubbornly.

"Because you've got my baby inside of you. You're not wasting another minute without being officially mine."

***

Six hours later, I had her on her back in my bed.

I was slowly working my length in and out of her, letting her feel all of me as I drove my cock into her.

"Who do you belong to?" I whispered to her.

"You," she whispered back.

"I fucking love you."

She smiled.

"I fucking love you right back."

I lifted her legs to get as deep as I could and watched as my hard length filled her.

Slow and steady. In and out.

She was wet for me, so fuckin' wet.

Her eyes were half-closed, and her mouth was slightly opened as she panted.

"Hurry," she whispered.

"Yes, Mrs. Amsel. Anything for the bride on her wedding night."

She smiled.

The smile, however, quickly fell off her face as her orgasm overtook her, sweeping her down into a current so deep that she couldn't find her way back up again.

Seeing her let go like that set me off, and I poured my release inside of her, filling her so full that I wasn't sure she'd ever get me out of her completely ever again.

"I think you've broken me," she informed me a few minutes later as I cleaned her up.

I grinned and dropped a kiss down to her forehead, and then moved down her body until my face was even with her belly.

"I'm so fucking happy I could burst," I told her.

"You and me both, baby. You and me both."

ABOUT THE AUTHOR

Lani Lynn Vale is married to the love of her life that she met in high school. She fell in love with him because he was wearing baseball pants. Ten years later they have three perfectly crazy children and a cat named Demon who likes to wake her up at ungodly times in the night. They live in the greatest state in the world, Texas. She writes contemporary and romantic suspense, and has a love for all things romance. You can find Lani in front of her computer writing away in her fictional characters' world...that is until her husband and kids demand sustenance in the form of food and drink.

Manufactured by Amazon.ca
Bolton, ON

27153267R00157